Love is
a time of enchantment:
in it all days are fair and all fields
green. Youth is blest by it,
old age made benign:
the eyes of love see
roses blooming in December,
and sunshine through rain. Verily
is the time of true-love
a time of enchantment — and
Oh! how eager is woman
to be bewitched!

GALLIARD'S HAY

After her father's death, Perditta Fox, goddaughter of Elizabeth I, is forced to live with her uncle. Cold and tyrannical, he is determined to let nothing stand in the way of his treacherous plot to put Mary Stuart, a Catholic, on the throne of England. Perditta, loyal to her Queen, must find a way to thwart this plot and in so doing comes to a head-on confrontation with the dashing and ruthless Conn Galliard, her uncle's accomplice. Perditta is sworn to hate Conn, but as hate turns to love, she finds both her allegiance and her life in jeopardy.

Books by Clare Rossiter
Published by The House of Ulverscroft:

JACOBITE SUMMER
THREE SEASONS AT ASKRIGG

CLARE ROSSITER

GALLIARD'S HAY

Complete and Unabridged

ULVERSCROFT
Leicester

First published in the
United States of America

First Large Print Edition
published 1997

British Library CIP Data

Rossiter, Clare
    Galliard's Hay.—Large print ed.—
Ulverscroft large print series: romance
1. Love stories
2. Large type books
I. Title
823.9'14 [F]

ISBN 0–7089–3818–3

Published by
F. A. Thorpe (Publishing) Ltd.
Anstey, Leicestershire
Set by Words & Graphics Ltd.
Anstey, Leicestershire
Printed and bound in Great Britain by
T. J. International Ltd., Padstow, Cornwall

This book is printed on acid-free paper

1

I SWUNG away from the window and stared at the man in the Queen's livery.

"Do you know what is in this letter?" I demanded angrily, crumpling the thick paper between my fingers as I spoke.

Sir Robert Varley nodded gravely, his eyes quiet and purposeful and I realized that with such knowledge, he was no common messenger.

"Doubtless Her Majesty has her reasons," he said.

His calmness infuriated me and I crushed the offending letter against my skirts. "Why may I not marry the man my father chose for me?" I cried. "He thought to leave me safe and settled with a man he trusted and knew well."

"I can understand your feelings, but in this matter I must warn you that the Queen will not be disobeyed."

"But what can it matter to her whom I marry?" I burst out.

"You are Her Majesty's godchild," Sir Robert reminded me and I fell silent at his words.

I had seen Queen Elizabeth but once, which was odd considering the fact that she was my Godmother and sent me a pearl every New Year to prove it. We had heard that she was to make a progress to Bristol and would pass close by our house on her way. Although I was only ten at the time, I can still clearly recall the look my parents exchanged at the news; even then I realized that it was oddly wary and speculative. Looking back I suppose that they had fallen from favour and wondered whether to remain obscure or to put themselves forward. They must have decided on the latter, for I was dressed in a new gown of green velvet and put to wait at the gates in the hopes of presenting Her Majesty with a nosegay gathered from our gardens.

I had grown weary of waiting and had returned to the shade of the tree to make a daisy chain, when the maid called that the first riders were in sight, and forgetting to remove my floral decorations in my haste, I ran forward, stumbling with sudden shyness as the glorious being on the white horse turned her long, shrewd eyes towards me.

Even in that colourful, glittering multitude, I had no doubt which was the Queen. Dressed in a green gown not unlike my own in colour, she had a presence that shone above all others, announcing plainly that here was England personified.

Seeing the posy in my hot hand, she smiled and reined in her horse, bending over the mount's neck and calling to me loudly. Quite forgetting the verse I had learned, I ran forward and held out my offering, remembering belatedly to sink into a deep curtsey.

"Your name, child?" she asked. "I swear it should be Amaryllis or Helen with a countenance such as yours."

"No, Madam," I answered, childishly, indignant at the courtiers' knowing smiles. "It is Perditta — the lost one, my father says."

She drew back at my words as though I had struck her, and I looked wonderingly up as she searched my face, her own suddenly still and dazed. "Our compliments to your parents, child," she said at last. "Tell them that England has need of such offspring as you."

With those words, she flicked her reins and the long procession moved off, followed by my curious gaze, with the riders, intent upon their own business, sparing me no more than cursory glances.

"What did she say?" A hand touched my shoulder and I looked up to see my mother had left the shelter of the gatehouse where she had been hovering all morning.

I was puzzled. "That England had need of me," I mumbled. "She said to tell you that. What did she mean?"

My mother was silent and I wriggled uncomfortably as her fingers tightened. "That you will grow up," she said at last, "and be a woman to bear sons who will live and work for our country."

Sir Robert coughed discreetly behind me and I returned from memories of the past to the unhappy present. "Yes, I am Her Majesty's godchild," I said harshly. "I have but seen her once — and now she refuses consent for me to marry the man of my father's choice and forbids

4

me even to come to court. God's Faith, Sir, I had expected better treatment!"

"Her Majesty has reasons — "

I turned on him. "Do you know them?"

He smiled at my anger, but shook his head. "My Mistress is discreet," he commented. "I will say this, that Master Daubney, your betrothed, makes no secret of his religion. He is a Catholic, and as such not to be linked with Her Majesty's godchild."

"I am a good Protestant," I said quickly, "and he has sworn not to influence my faith."

"Nevertheless it is not to be — "

"Then what is to become of me?" I cried, taking a turn about the room in my impatience, my heels tapping on the wooden floor. "In her letter the Queen forbids me even to present myself at Court and my father's nephew comes shortly to take up his inheritance here."

"You cannot make a home with him?"

"No," I answered shortly and turned away to hide the hot blush that glared in my cheeks at the thought of the many times I had eluded Cousin John's hot hands or fought off his unwelcome kisses. "He is married and — not to my liking."

"Her Majesty suggests that you should accept your uncle at Hawks' Hill as guardian."

I looked at him, not liking the hint of an order behind his words. "He would not take kindly to having a penniless female foisted upon him."

"I see," he returned my look, reaching inside his doublet for a carefully folded and sealed parchment, which he placed on the table in front of me. "In that case you had best read this, mistress."

Slowly I picked it up and examined it, recognizing my father's seal and elegant writing. The thick parchment crackled under my fingers as I broke the wax and spread out the single sheet. I read quickly at first, making no sense of the legal jargon, then forced myself to return to the heading and read more slowly, taking in the meaning. Slowly sinking down into a chair, I dropped the letter on to the gleaming table top and stared silently before me.

"Do you know what it is?" I asked,

my voice echoing around the room.

"Master Fox's will."

By this time I knew no surprise at the extent of his knowledge. "He leaves me everything — except the house for that is entailed upon my cousin." I flicked the parchment with one finger. "A sum of five thousand pounds is mentioned."

"You are an heiress, Mistress Fox."

The glance I sent him would have withered a lesser mortal. "My father was a scholar, Sir Robert, and such, as you must know, are notoriously poor. My father could not have left me five pounds! The will is a fake — a cruel hoax, a joke that you have lent yourself to."

"Study it," he advised calmly. "I take it that you are familiar with your father's signature."

Reluctantly, I smoothed out the folded paper and carried it to the window for a better examination. There could be no doubt about the careful, elegant signature, only my father wrote in just such a hand and the witnesses were those of our steward and the lawyer who had journeyed out from Bristol so often of late. "But where did the money come from?" I asked.

The man beside me shrugged. "A merchant venture perhaps. Perhaps he had a share in a privateer and was reluctant for you to know. Accept it, Mistress, and be grateful."

I took exception to his dry tone and answered bitterly "We could have put it to good use. We needed comforts while he was alive. These last few months I would have given much to be able to pay for a better physician and nourishing foods."

"To deny himself such, he must have wanted you to have it very much. Take it gratefully as a last gift from him."

"It would certainly make me more welcome in my Uncle Campernowne's home — had I any intention of going there."

"I must remind you that Her Majesty's wishes are always commands," Sir Robert said pleasantly.

"But why? I don't even know my uncle. Save that my mother thought him miserly, I know nothing about him. We have never met. Why are you so sure he will accept my presence?"

"Her Majesty can be very pressing."

"Then all is arranged — and without my consultation? What if I refuse?"

"Let us say that would not be wise."

His quiet words hung in the air and while inwardly I seethed with helpless anger, outwardly I acquiesced. My father had been very liberal in his views of female emancipation and had treated me as the son he had never had. I had been allowed to refuse suitors and even Tom Daubney had been of my own choosing. He, poor man, had seemed an easy way out of a difficult situation and I had picked him as one who would allow me my own way much as my father had. Unused as I was to being constrained, I found that I had no liking for being treated as a pawn. However, my intelligence told me that to make an enemy of Queen Elizabeth could be only foolishness and I bowed my head. "When do we start?" I asked submissively.

"I had wondered if your commonsense would outweigh your temper," observed Sir Robert laconically and as I looked up quickly, he gestured to my hair. "I have learned to be wary of that precise shade," he said. "Her Majesty's colouring is much the same as yours."

I touched my smooth, auburn hair, pleased that he had noticed my one pride. Not a beauty, I had only the one thing to commend me and even as a child had known a thrill of pride as my mother brushed my hair and said fondly that any lady at Court would have envied me the colour that the Queen had made fashionable. Hiding my pleasure, I enquired again when we would leave.

"I have business in Bristol which will take several days and give you time to assemble a wardrobe. I shall return in a week, Mistress."

I thought he winced as his eyes travelled over my morning gown that had first been my mother's and knew that he was tactfully suggesting that some of my new wealth should be put to use at once. As though reading my thoughts, he produced a heavy purse and set it on the table by my hand. "An advance upon Master Fox's will," he said. "I believe the rest will be sent to Master Campernowne's house in Hampshire."

With sudden understanding, I realized that only if I agreed to my uncle's guardianship would I receive the money and could not stop my eyebrows from shooting upwards.

"Precisely," he said, meaningly. "I take it we have reached an understanding." Before I could think of a suitable retort, he bowed low and marched from the room, his short velvet cloak swinging, the thick gold thread that edged it glinting richly in the gathering dusk.

Hurriedly penning a note to Tom Daubney, I sent it by messenger and waited for the reply. When the next day passed without an answer I knew that Sir Robert had also called at the Daubney estate, doubtless speaking his calm threats into Tom's ear with as great an effect as he had in me. When my betrothed's letter finally came, it was a masterpiece of circumspection, saying all that was necessary and regretting that due to ill health he would be unable to see me before I left for Hampshire.

While realizing that Master Daubney was far from a hero of romance, I had expected better than this and, stifling my resentment that he obviously so little regretted losing me as a bride, I turned my attention to refurbishing my wardrobe, no easy matter when the only available material was that which remained of my mother's clothes. I settled this difficulty by sending a groom into Bristol to one of the cloth merchants there, desiring him to send back a selection of his best materials and within a day or two I and my maids were busy cutting and stitching.

Having very rarely bought new materials for myself I delighted in arranging a wardrobe fit for an heiress, finding pleasure in choosing satins and brocades and hesitating between tawny velvet or patterned damask.

When Sir Robert returned, mainly to accent my independence, I told him that I was not ready and kept him drumming his heels for a few days before I admitted to readiness. Finally, accompanied by the Queen's men and my maid, I left the only home I had ever known and set out along the dusty road for my new life in Hampshire.

The early morning sun was shining

brightly and from the branches of a nearby tree a blackbird sang as I turned to take a last farewell of my home. From the vantage point of the rising road I could see the house set out at my feet, the colours clear and fresh. One of the maids was hanging the wash on the hedges to dry, and as I watched, the wagon carrying my new wardrobe trundled under the gatehouse. Suddenly an air of anticipation filled me; my life which I had expected to be usual and mundane had suddenly altered. Ahead of me lay a meeting with kinsmen whom I had never known, new surroundings to be explored and new acquaintances to be made. Turning my horse, I plunged after the others coming up with Sir Robert, whom I expected had waited for me at the crest of the hill.

"Are you not sorry to leave your father's house?" he asked, seeing my flushed cheeks and sparkling eyes.

Falling into step beside him, I considered his question. "My parents made it home," I told him. "With them gone . . . it is just a house. I have my memories to take with me and I'd prefer to be far away before my Cousin John arrives."

"You do not like him?"

"I dislike him! He has creeping, nipping fingers and wet lips and seems to believe that I should find them both irresistible!"

Sir Robert laughed. "But surely your father could have protected you."

"If I had made the matter known to him — but you see my cousin has a gentle little wife, forever bearing babes, who looks at him with doe-like eyes and imagines him a god. I could have no part in disillusioning her," I told him briefly and looking ahead changed the subject. "How long shall we be on the road?"

Wide shoulders rose and fell in an expansive shrug. "Who knows? God willing, three or four days should see us at Hawk's Hill, but should the weather turn bad, or the roads be impassable, then we may take a week . . . and if we should meet with highwaymen — " He shrugged again and left the sentence unfinished, glancing at me out of the corner of his eye to see what effect his statement had had.

"I believe you are trying to frighten

me," I told him roundly, "but I have no fear of robbers." I patted the dagger at my waist, serviceable and deadly for all its decorated hilt and slender blade. "Toledo steel," I said confidently, "and my father had a swordsman teach me how to use it."

"How very thoughtful of him," Sir Robert commented. "I wonder what can have persuaded him of the need? Is Somerset more unlawful than I thought?"

"I suppose he wished me to be safe," I said shortly, wondering a little myself. Now that it had been brought to my notice, such violence seemed unlikely in my quiet scholarly father.

"Where do we stay the night?" I asked after a while.

"Warminster," answered the man beside me, but his manner was preoccupied and as he seemed unwilling for conversation, I kicked my heel into my horse's side and rode ahead.

Mary, my maid, rode pillion behind one of the grooms, while Sir Robert's two men trotted in the lead. As I came up, they parted to allow me to ride a little ahead of them, but I noticed that

15

they were careful not to fall more than a pace behind.

We ate our midday meal of bread and cheese beside the road, while the horses drank from a stream and then we mounted and cantered on again, riding into Warminster as the spring sun was losing its warmth and purple shadows were beginning to creep under trees.

The inn followed the old custom of hanging a green branch above the door, making the men duck their heads as they entered. The landlord received us, bowing and smiling obsequiously enough to make me take instant dislike, but the chamber offered to Mary and myself was clean and comfortable enough and the table his wife set was better than that in many private houses.

Sir Robert and I dined in private while sounds of jollity carried from the kitchens, where the men and Mary were eating their evening meal. The Queen's messenger looked up and frowned, turning his head in the direction of a sudden burst of laughter.

"I can vouch for my men," he said. "I hope you can do the same for the

16

discretion of your maid."

"Of course", I said shortly, "though why the morals of my servant should bother you puzzles me somewhat."

He snapped his fingers. "A fig for your wench's virtue! I was thinking of highwaymen." My eyes opened and he nodded grimly at my startled expression.

"Some robber bands are in league with the landlords of inns and pay for information about the road to be taken by travellers. If your maid should make free with our direction, we could find an unpleasant surprise awaiting us."

"I am sure she would not be so foolish," I said, stoutly, but inwardly felt very far from certain and the minute we retired for the night and were alone, I rounded on her. "Mary, have you spoken about our destination?" I asked, as she took the pins out of my hair.

"Lord, Miss, who'd I talk to about such a thing?" she said, comfortably, beginning to brush my hair. "The men all know where we're agoing."

"So you haven't told anyone at the inn?" The brush faltered and she shook her head uncertainly, while I caught my breath. "The landlord — he wondered if we had far to go and I did say I heard Sir Robert saying he hoped to be in Salisbury tomorrow." She looked at me hopefully. "Where's the harm, Miss? The landlord seems a goodly man and eager to help."

I sighed and, remembering my denial, decided to say nothing to our escort. "We'll pray no harm has been done," I told her. "Sir Robert, for all his brave air, is, I fear, an old woman and sees danger where there is none." With this comforting thought, I went to bed, but later the next day I was to regret my rash act and wish I had confided in the man who rode beside me.

Having passed the great house at Wilton, we were riding on, replete after the midday meal and somnolent under the warmth of the sun, when I was jerked awake by the actions of a group of men as they galloped out of a thick copse ahead. Before I could do more than exclaim and touch Sir Robert's arm, they charged us, waving sticks and cudgels and uttering wild shouts.

The surprise of their attack divided

us and I found myself on the edge of the fray while the horsemen manoeuvred their mounts the better to reach their opponents. As Mary tumbled from her pillion and ran for the cover of a bush, the sound of wood on flesh, jingling accoutrements and the gasps and grunts of fighting men and the snorts of frightened horses filled the air. Looking about for help, I saw the long empty road stretching across the flat plain and knew that no aid would be forthcoming.

The group broke up into individual fights and to my dismay my escort seemed to be getting the worst of it. Sir Robert was beset by two ruffians, while my own groom crouched in his saddle, protecting his head with his arms, having given up all attempts to defend himself as a man twice his age beat him savagely with a short wooden stave.

Sudden rage at the unprovoked attack filled me and shouting to Mary to hand me a cudgel that lay discarded by the bush, I snatched it from her fingers and charged into battle. The large fellow must have had a weak head for one blow laid him low.

Unfortunately, the cudgel developed a life of its own and wrenched itself from my fingers, flying straight up into the air. However, in its downward path, it struck one of our attacker's mounts between the ears, causing it to shy and throw its rider, so I counted it well lost and having tasted blood, looked about for more deeds to be done. Sir Robert was hard pressed by his two opponents; even as I looked, one crept under his guard and thrust his sword into his shoulder. Kicking my heels into my horse, I rode forward, remembering the dagger at my side for the first time. Seeing that the Queen's man seemed able to deal with one of the robbers, I gave my attention to the other, choosing my place well as I had been taught and waiting until the target presented itself, before reaching forward and cutting my dagger deep into the thick arm muscle of the man who was warily circling Sir Robert, waiting for a place to strike.

With a screech, he dropped his weapon and clutched his arm before, swaying in the saddle, he lost interest in the fight and rode away. With the loss of their leader the others abandoned hope of robbing us and as suddenly as they had come were gone, riding into the woods and quietly vanishing as though they had never been. Only my groaning groom and the heaving chests of my escort showed proof that they had ever been.

"Well, what a little fighting bird we have here," said Sir Robert behind me, a hint of laughter in his voice. "They should have been wary of that red hair."

"It's good for you that I was armed," I reminded him, shortly.

"True," he admitted and sketched a bow over the pommel. "My thanks, Mistress Fox." The smile faded from his face, leaving it white and strained as slowly his head fell forward.

"Quickly," I called, clutching at his arm to save him from falling. "Your Master needs aid."

His men ran forward at my shout and soon he was laid on the grass, his doublet stripped from him and his shoulder laid bare. Viewing the welling blood with disfavour, I looked around to find all eyes on me and knew that I was expected to deal with the emergency. My mother had taught me simple first aid and I had dealt with many a cut finger or lost nail, but never before had I been called upon to attend a wound caused by a sword.

Reluctantly I knelt beside the prone man and gingerly examined his shoulder. To my relief the blade seemed to have been deflected by the bone of his shoulder and the wound was little more than a deep cut. Mary had produced my box of herbs and liniments which I had had the forethought to bring and I spread some salve over the wound and bound it tightly with strips of linen.

Sir Robert seemed to have been unconscious for some time and I sent his men for water from a convenient stream, while I anxiously felt his brow. Bending nearer I smoothed back his hair. Thinking his eyelashes flickered against his brown cheek, I peered closer and surprised a quiver on his lips.

"You are awake!" I accused, sitting up.

"Alas," he moaned, "I had hoped to be awakened like Sleeping Beauty, by a kiss."

Hastily removing myself out of his

reach I eyed him sternly. "And I detect a delirium. I shall mix you a brew to cool the blood," I told him severely.

"Eye of toad and leg of newt?" he asked.

"Nothing like — but it will taste as horrid."

His hand covered mine. "I have an idea that I did not manage to thank you properly," he said, the laughter leaving his voice. Lifting my hand he carried it to his mouth and brushed my fingers with his lips.

Voices sounded behind us. I quickly removed my hand from his grasp and rose to my feet, feeling it best to leave bold Sir Robert to the ministrations of others. Having advised a mixture of wine and water, I retired to a chair. The invalid drank the beverage with obvious distaste, asked for help with his doublet, and struggled unaided back into his saddle. "Is this wise?" I asked, shading my eyes against the sun as I peered up at him. "Let one of your men go for aid. Salisbury cannot be far."

"Neither, Mistress, are the band of ruffians who attacked us. Even now, they may be watching from the shelter of those trees".

Involuntarily I shivered and glanced quickly over my shoulder to the thicket that had hidden them before. Struck by the sense of his words, I mounted without further demure and we cantered away from the scene of our unexpected adventure.

Soon the spire of Salisbury rose out of the flat fields ahead and we rode on with lightened hearts. I had watched Sir Robert with anxious eyes, for all he appeared little the worse for his wound, and knew a measure of relief at the thought of safe lodgings and welcoming care at some inn in the little town where we would stay the night.

After dinner, Sir Robert, instead of retiring to nurse his shoulder as I had expected, suggested that he and I should take the evening air and explore a little of the town. Thinking that he was old enough to know his own limitations, I accepted, the more eagerly as I was wearing one of my new gowns and was especially willing to show it off. Placing my fingers elegantly in his, I allowed him to lead me from the inn, pleased rather than otherwise with the stares and interest we aroused as we paraded the street. The market square was still busy and I could well understand that now their day's work was done, the townsfolk were reluctant to leave the pleasant evening and return to their houses for the night.

As we left the square an altercation arose behind us and suddenly a man plunged past, thrusting me aside so violently that but for Sir Robert's arm, I would have fallen. Before he could do more than push me against the safety of a wall and protect me with his body, a shouting, gesticulating crowd ran after the man. Shaken by the ugly emotion shown on their faces, I turned my face against the velvet doublet in front of me, afraid of what I would see if they caught the fugitive. "W-was he a thief?" I asked, when they had gone. I shook out my skirts with an assumption of calm I was very far from feeling.

Sir Robert released me, but I noticed he was still alert and watchful. "I think not, sweetheart," he answered thoughtfully.

"They seemed to be calling him both Spaniard and spy."

"It's true he was very dark of visage." He took my arm and we began to walk back to our lodgings. "And so are many honest Englishmen."

"I find it strange that these townsfolk should have supposed a spy in their midst. I have lived so far from London that any news I heard was old and out of date. Have there been new plots or rumours of which I have yet to hear?"

Sir Robert looked down at me, his expression serious for once. "The Spanish and Jesuits are always at some campaign or other," he said simply, but with conviction. "This very spring comes news of the so-called Enterprise of England — a new plot devised by the Pope and various Catholic princes to set Mary Stuart upon the throne of England."

"But how do you know?" I could not help asking.

He laughed shortly. "Walsingham has a network of spies himself, so vast and efficient that Her Majesty vows she knows more about the plots than does King Philip himself. A priest was

26

taken and a letter on him told much, even though the poor man tore it up and threw it overboard as the vessel was taken — unfortunately the wind blew the pieces back again."

I eyed him coldly. "You should write plays, Sir Robert," I said. "You have the talent for it".

"God's teeth, I swear it's the truth!" he cried, torn between amusement and exasperation at my disbelief of his story.

He would have detained me further, but as we had reached the inn by this time, I bade him a cool 'goodnight' and slipping under his arm, ran upstairs to the chamber Mary and I shared.

Although I had rejected his outrageous tale, something in his manner told me that it was not altogether untrue, and I was uneasy at the thought of plot and counter-plot that must go on while most of England was unaware of such happenings. While brought up a Protestant, neither I nor my parents had been fanatics — our religion was a warm, comforting thing; we had no wish to impose our views on others and could not understand those who did.

27

The thought of another Catholic Mary on the throne and a return to the religious persecutions of the last reign made my sleep uneasy and filled with wild, frightening dreams. Awakening from one nightmare, I heard rain beating loudly against the little panes of the lattice window and knew that the weather had broken. Sighing for the journey we would have on the morrow, I turned my face into the pillow and resolutely shut my mind to all save pleasant things and so by an effort fell at last into a dreamless sleep.

2

WE breakfasted on beef and ale while rain continued to fall from a sullen sky. Having viewed the wet street and dripping houses from my window, I expected to spend the day at the inn and so was not a little surprised when Sir Robert appeared booted and cloaked and obviously prepared to set out.

"Surely you do not intend to ride out in such weather?" I asked, incredulously.

"A little rain won't hurt you, sweetheart," he said, cheerfully. "I've heard 'tis good for the complexion."

"And chills and colds," I answered crossly.

"The roads will not be too bad at the moment — and if we wait, we could find them impassible," he said reasonably.

I have never liked being reasoned with and hunched a shoulder as I pointedly turned and stared out of the window. "Whatever the state of the roads, Sir

Robert," I said firmly, "I refuse to journey forth until the rain stops."

"My dear Mistress Fox," he said, hurrying forward to take my hand, his voice anxious, "I had not realized that our little fracas of yesterday had so upset you. Of course delicate females cannot be expected to regard such happenings with the equanimity of a man. I should have realized that your nerve would fail you."

"There is nothing wrong with my nerve — I do not want to get wet!"

He bowed gracefully. "I accept your excuse," he said kindly and meeting his eyes, I knew that I was defeated. With a few well chosen words, Sir Robert Varley had beaten me. To save my pride I tied the strings of my safeguard round my waist to protect my skirt and rode out, with as good a grace as I could muster, into the hated rain.

We ate our luncheon in the shelter of a barn and then hurried on, growing short-tempered and morose under the continuing onslaught of the rain. My skirt was mired to the waist and the wet had soaked through my cloak to send icy droplets down my back. Drips fell from the sodden brim of my hat, trickling down my face to join the puddle in my lap. Glaring across at Sir Robert, I saw with satisfaction that he was in no better state and meeting his gaze gave him a cool smile which I thought expressed my thoughts adequately.

"Are you snarling at me?" he asked with interest.

"If I was it would be no more than you deserve," I retorted bitterly. "As a weather prophet, let me tell you, you are singularly untalented!"

"We'll stop at the next inn," he promised.

For a while I rode on in a glow of expectation, but as the road remained empty of all signs of habitation, soon came to suspect that the Queen's Messenger had travelled that way before and knew full well that the next inn we would come upon would be at the end of a day's hard ride. Sure enough, not until we reached Winchester did we see the welcome sight of a resting place.

"You planned this," I hissed as he lifted me down. "You had no intention of stopping until we reached this God forsaken town."

Sir Robert appeared hurt and put one hand on his heart. "Mistress, upon my word of honor, had we come upon a lodging house, we would have taken refuge there."

"But you knew that the road was empty, did you not?" I asked, twitching my soaking skirt out of the dirty puddles on the cobbled yard.

"If you stay here, you will only get wetter," he pointed out gently and as though to point to the truth of his words, the weather made a fresh onslaught.

With a muttered exclamation I ducked my head and ran for shelter.

The next morning I awoke and lay in the unfamiliar bed listening, but hearing only the sweet sounds of song birds, realized that the rain had stopped. Relief and something like excitement began to fill me; with luck and no untoward happenings, we would arrive at Hawk's Hill later that day and I would meet for the first time my uncle's unknown family.

I stared in dismay at my kirtle and

bodice that had been dried overnight beside the kitchen fire. The soft velvet was crisp and hard, the subtle colour streaked and faded, and I realized that I would make my arrival in a style far from that which I had intended.

However, interest in my unfamiliar surroundings soon drove all thought of my appearance from my mind and as I rode, I looked from side to side, taking in the lush, rounded downs of the Hampshire countryside. The rain seemed to have washed everything clean and the meadows and hedges glistened and sparkled. The building materials were different to those of my hometown of Somerset. Here, I noted with interest, flints were used to build the cottage walls. One glance into the fields that lined the road told me where they came from, and I spared a moment's sympathy for the farmer's labours as he ploughed his flinty furrows.

The rain of yesterday had settled the dust that covered the road and we travelled without the usual discomfort of having ourselves and our mounts covered in a fine dirt film. As we journeyed on, between wooded slopes that pressed close against the road, I noticed that Sir Robert and his men grew wary, loosening their swords in their sheaths and glancing from side to side.

"Do we expect attack?" I asked.

Sir Robert hardly spared me a glance, his attention on the road and thick trees ahead.

"The Pass of Alton is notorious," he answered briefly. "Highwaymen and robbers have made their home in these forests for years. I had hoped to meet up with other travellers before this and so ride on together, presenting a more formidable party, but as it is, we'll have to hope that the Queen's livery will give them pause."

He called to his men to throw back their cloaks and show the Queen's device on their chests. I felt an uneasy prickling between my shoulder blades and rode nervously until we turned off the main road. Not until we had left the danger far behind was I able to relax.

We passed scattered hamlets and a valley which had supported a Priory until some years previously. The buildings were in ruins now, most of the stone having been carried away to make humbler dwellings. At last we came upon my uncle's house. I stared a while at the new, timbered building beneath its hat of thatch, impressed by its size and newness. Then I kicked my heels into my horse's side and caught up with Sir Robert, where he had waited for me.

"It's very fine," I commented.

He must have sensed my nervousness for he smiled over his shoulder at me. "Remember you are an heiress," he said bracingly, "and as such doubly welcome to your mother's brother."

Somewhat to my surprise I found I was expected, people appearing in the doorway and coming out to greet us as soon as Sir Robert's two men rode into the courtyard.

"Welcome, welcome!" cried an overweight man in brown velvet, bowing ceremoniously before he hurried down the steps towards us.

"The Queen was sure of my obeying her wish," I observed dryly to Sir Robert as he lifted me down from my horse.

35

"Her Majesty's wish is everyone else's command," he murmured for my ear alone, as he set me on my feet and turned to present me to my uncle.

"Mistress Perditta Fox," he said smoothly, making a most elegant leg, one hand on the hilt of his sword.

My uncle raised me from my curtsey. "My dear child," he said, having kissed me heartily, "how I have waited for this day! To see my sister's daughter for the first time — and grown to womanhood. Let me present my family."

Surreptitiously I wiped my cheek. My uncle's kiss had been over moist, reminding me strangely of my amorous kinsman from Somerset, and I tried to dispel the first feelings of dislike my mother's brother had aroused in me. I found my aunt Campernowne to be a large woman, towering over her family and myself alike. Her son Dudley, a big florid youth, dressed like a popinjay and trying unsuccessfully to ape Sir Robert's ease of manner, was easily recognisable as his parents' favourite, but his sister Jane was more to my liking. For all she appeared shy and diffident, her eyes when they met mine were friendly and intelligent.

Sir Robert was pressed to stay the night and in the general noise and bustle, Jane appeared quietly at my side offering to take me to my chamber. Master Campernowne was shouting instructions in a voice more befitting to the quarter deck of a ship than a country house. Later I was to discover this was his usual manner; my uncle I realized was a bully and sought to make his presence known and his wishes obeyed by a show of confidence that overrode all other considerations. Sir Robert, I was glad to see, seemed unimpressed, appearing to become more remote with each onslaught of my uncle's raucous tones.

"Nay, girl," he cried loudly as Jane led me up the wide stairs. "We have servants to do that."

Pausing on the lower steps, one hand on the balustrade, I turned back to the company, aware that my cousin Jane had flushed unbecomingly at her father's words.

"Why, Uncle," I said, pitching my voice to carry across the hall, "I take it as a compliment that my cousin escorts me herself."

For a moment our eyes met and I saw that his full face was brightly mottled, either with excitement or anger, I could not tell which. I saw his eyes narrow and I thought he would order his daughter back as his complexion darkened, but then he seemed to recollect his other guest. He turned back to the Queen's Messenger with a shrug, dismissing Jane and myself as of little importance.

Jane sighed audibly with relief and putting a hand on my arm, urged me up the shallow stairs and along a wide passage to a room at the back of the house.

"I thought you'd like it here," she said, hesitantly, opening the door to reveal a chamber flooded with evening sunlight. "It looks out over the fields — and as you see, catches the sun."

The bedhangings were white linen, alive with exotic animals and flowers, worked in bright colours. "It's beautiful," I exclaimed, walking into the middle of the room. "So new and bright."

She nodded, pouring water into a basin

for me to wash away the dust of travel. "My father built the house. We only moved in a year ago." She looked down suddenly and her cheeks grew flushed again. "You must take no notice of his manner," she said, uncomfortably. "He is a merchant, as you know, and as such is used to ordering people and being obeyed."

I said nothing, thinking of my own quiet father and suspecting that my Uncle Campernowne and I would not agree. To change the subject I began relating the adventures of our journey and was pleased to feel that the basis of a friendship had been shown by the time Mary, my maid, arrived with my travelling trunk to set out my clothes for dinner.

Sir Robert Varley left for London and I set about the task of settling into my new home, though I suspected that my presence was not as welcome as my kinsmen wished me to believe. Upon closer acquaintance my uncle did not improve; with Sir Robert gone he felt no need to curb his tongue or temper. While, so far, I had not found myself the recipient of his wrath, I felt it best to remove myself from his presence as much as possible.

My aunt was a cold, austere woman, totally taken up with the business of running her large establishment. Dudley appeared harmless, but quite devoid of interest or intelligence. He was indulged by his parents upon every account, while Jane, who in my opinion was worth two of him, was either ignored or derided. Often I burned with anger on her account at some slight or hurt, but she seemed impervious, only the ready flush betraying her emotions as she hung her head under her mother's sharp tongue or accepted a quick cuff from the heavy hand of her father.

"How can you be so quiet and docile?" I asked, one day, tried beyond endurance by her father's petty tempers. "I would — " At a loss for words, I spread my hands in a helpless gesture.

"My dear Perditta, it would avail me nothing. I learnt as a child that a show of spirit brought me nothing more than a beating or a week in my chamber."

I was aghast at her revelations. "I have

heard of such things, but hardly believed them true."

She smiled slightly. "Your childhood seems like a fairy story to me," she pointed out gently, before her face grew troubled. "I only hope that you and my father don't clash."

"I'll do my best," I told her briefly.

"I've seen you hold back a retort many a time, but my father is not an insensitive man. He must realize how you feel . . . For all your connections, I fear he will not suffer a rebellion in his household. He will take much from Dudley, but very little from anyone else."

She sighed and looked away, continuing with her needlework, while I returned to a question that had bothered me for some time.

"Forgive me for asking," I said at last, "but why have you not married? You are presentable enough to please any man. I have seen how good a housewife and needlewoman you are . . . it would have been a way of escape from what can hardly be a happy life here."

Her needle ceased to flash in and out

of the material and for a few seconds her hands were idle, then she resumed her work. "There are reasons," she said painfully. "My father has not found any of my suitors acceptable . . . I pray you, do not ask me why. I would not have it so, but there is something which must remain a secret from you."

I blinked at her in astonishment and fell silent, pondering upon this dread secret that belonged to my quiet peaceful cousin . . . or was it my uncle himself, I suddenly wondered, who harbored some hidden scandal or shame? Out of kindness to Jane, I declined to question her further, but with my mind more alert to puzzles, suddenly became aware of an air of secrecy which prevailed in the house from time to time.

Several times as spring gave way to summer, I came upon strangers in the house. At first I took them for servants, but as I became accustomed to the members of the household, I grew more certain that I did not recognize them. Another aspect which puzzled me was the speed with which these strangers vanished; one day they were there,

I would encounter them upon the stairs or meet them in the corridor, and as suddenly they were gone. At least I would presume them gone, for I would see them no more. Another thing which interested me was the atmosphere of suppressed excitement which filled Hawks' Hill when they were there. Aunt Campernowne wore an air of satisfaction, which reminded me forcibly of a cat who had found the dairy door open, while Jane grew nervous, starting like a hunted deer at the slightest unexpected noise.

"Good Heavens, what ails you?" I cried, losing my patience as she jumped to her feet at the sound of hooves clattering across the yard, scattering her sewing materials about the polished floor. "It's only Dudley returning from some expedition. Whom do you expect? You behave as though the Devil himself might come acalling."

She smiled slightly and bent to help me pick up her thread and needle. "It's the weather," she excused herself, "I never care for the heat, it makes my head ache." Her voice was composed, but I noticed her hand shook as she returned to her embroidery.

"Let me make a tisane," I suggested. "A herb drink will be sure to ease your head."

"My mother keeps the key to the stillroom."

"I'll ask for it," I offered, thinking to understand her reluctance.

"She would want to know the reason and then I would be chided for my stupidity." She shook her head. "It's easier not to bother her."

"What nonsense!" I said, roundly. "What housewifery is this, that one must go short of a cure for the headache rather than bother your mother?"

"Oh, pray sit down, Cousin Perditta," Jane cried and at the genuine note of panic in her voice I obeyed. "Believe me it's better not to make a fuss. The headache will go . . . I've had them often enough to know how they will behave."

"I believe it's because you are upset," I said shrewdly. "My mother suffered so whenever she was worried."

"Perhaps — " she shrugged indifferently, turning back to her needlework. "Let us talk of something totally different

44

. . . something that has nothing whatever to do with Hawks' Hill. Tell me about your childhood and how you met the Queen."

She settled down like a child waiting for its favourite fairy tale and after a moment I began, realizing not for the first time as I did so, how lucky I had been in having parents such as mine.

"Why have you not wed?" she asked, when at last I ran out of anecdotes. "I am sure that parents such as yours would never have refused permission if your heart was set."

"No," I answered, slowly. "Neither would they force me where my heart was not." I laughed a little at her puzzled expression. "The truth is, dear cousin, that I never found a man I could wish to share my life with. I was happy with my books and the company of my father and his scholarly friends. Indeed, after my mother's death, I believe he forgot the need to find me a husband, until he was near death himself. Then his thoughts turned to Master Tom Daubney, a near neighbour of ours, but it was not to be. The Queen herself refused permission, so you see me a spinster still."

"You don't sound unhappy at the upset of your plans."

I considered. "I daresay he would have made a good husband, in the sense that he was wealthy and I would have been mistress of a large house."

"You did not care for him?"

"No."

Jane stared thoughtfully out of the window at the pleasant summer garden. A bumblebee flew noisily in at the window and buzzed busily round the room before he found his way out again. "I wonder why the Queen did not want you to wed?"

"I don't think she objected to my marrying, though Sir Robert says she can be very awkward about her maids of honour doing such a thing. I believe that it was the fact that Tom Daubney is a Catholic that she disliked."

Jane stared at me, her eyes wide and shadowed in her pale face. Before gathering up her materials with clumsy hands, she murmured that her head was so bad she must lie down and fled from the room, leaving me to wonder what I could have said to upset her.

Determined as I was to find the reason for her distress, all thoughts of the matter were driven from my head by the arrival of a house guest. I had seen him arrive from an upstairs window, my eyes widening at the magnificence of his mount and the splendour of his clothes. As though sensing my appraisal, he glanced up, meeting my gaze before I drew back into the shadows, my heart beating curiously fast as I hurried back to my chamber.

For some reason I chose to wear my best gown that evening, an olive green satin that set off the colour of my hair. As an afterthought, I slipped the chain with the pearls the Queen had given me each year over my head and surveying myself in the mirror was well pleased with the result; the tight stays made my waist elegantly small, while the farthingale held out my skirts like the bell of a flower.

My heart fluttered a little as I descended the stairs but I told myself it was with excitement rather than nervousness and held my head high. The man talking to my uncle watched as I approached, breaking off his conversation to touch the other on the arm, drawing his attention to my presence. My uncle looked none too pleased at the interruption and introduced me perfunctorily.

"Let me present my niece, Mistress Perditta Fox, who has lately come up from Somerset," he said curtly, as I sank into a curtsey.

"Sir Conn Galliard," said the stranger, matching my curtsey with an elaborate bow, taking my hand as I rose and conveying it to his lips. "Had I knowledge that Hampshire contained such beauty, I would not have stayed away so long," he went on gallantly.

"Have you been on a journey?"

"I've spent several years on the Continent."

"I hear it's a dangerous place."

"None so dangerous as here mistress, for never have I been like to lose my heart before."

"If you carry such an important item upon your sleeve, I fear it is easy to lose," I told him coolly and went to join Jane, who was standing quietly by the window.

The encounter had made me a little uneasy and I found it difficult to attend to her chatter, glancing surreptitiously over my shoulder at the man talking to my uncle. Dressed in black velvet with only an ornate silver chain about his shoulders to relieve the sombre effect, he made me think of the descriptions of the Spanish Grandees which I had heard. With his black curling hair and neat pointed beard he could have been a Spaniard or a pirate. I considered, wondering why he should both attract and repel me and had just decided that he had an air of ruthlessness which I disliked, when Jane touched my arm.

"Do you like him?" she asked.

"Who?"

"Our visitor — Sir Conn," she said, her eyes on the tall figure on the other side of the room.

"I hardly know . . . I think not," I answered slowly. "I think he is both arrogant and dangerous."

She lifted her eyes to my face and I was startled to read the fear in their depths. "I pray you are not right," she said quietly and moved away, leaving me to the attentions of her brother, who attempted to out-do Sir Conn, annoying and embarrassing me with his foolish efforts at gallantry.

Having dealt him a verbal box on the ears, I pointedly turned my shoulder and busied myself with examining a book of music that lay beside the virginals, placed ready on the table for Jane to show off her prowess after dinner.

Usually my uncle dominated the conversation around the long dining table, but this evening, Sir Conn took the lead and for the first time in months we did not have to listen to Harry Campernowne's monologue of self-congratulation. Dudley sat up with an air of interest and left off searching for my toe with his foot, Jane turned her quiet blue eyes upon the newcomer and even ventured an opinion while my aunt continued to consume her usual quantity of food, nodding solemn agreement to every statement as was her wont.

I had to admit that Sir Conn was a good conversationalist. His tales and anecdotes were enjoyable to all and yet he by no means dominated the conversation being skilled enough to make his companions feel witty and brilliant. Enjoying his talk and our verbal battles, I yet knew an unease in his presence; while he appeared contented and at ease, I felt that he was playing a part. The gaze he turned on all of us at times when he thought himself unnoticed seemed a shade too shrewd and watchful for that of a gentleman at dinner with friends.

However, no-one save myself appeared aware of his moments of detachment and I stifled my reservations, joining in the jollity after dinner with a free mind and a verve I had long thought lost.

Either the candles had made the room exceedingly hot or I had drank an excessive amount of wine, but having said 'goodnight' prior to retiring to my room, I stood at the bottom of the stairs, clinging to the carved, bulbous newel post, while the hall girated round me in a most unpleasant manner. Knowing I could never climb the stairs and unwilling to have anyone see me in such a condition, I fumbled my way out into the gardens, hoping that the night air would cool my hot head and burning cheeks.

Seating myself on the shallow steps of the terrace, I leaned my aching head against the stone balustrade and closed my eyes. It seemed I awoke only a few seconds later, but I discovered with dismay that the dew already lay damp on my gown and I started quickly to my feet, well aware that had my uncle locked the great door as was his custom each night, I would have to make an explanation for my behaviour.

Thankfully I saw the door still open and slipped quietly inside, rising on tiptoe as I hurried towards the stairs. Voices carried to me as I passed my uncle's study and I walked even more quietly, trying to stifle the whisper of my skirts.

One word spoken in my uncle's robust tones caught my attention and almost without volition on my part, I paused and leaning close to the door, listening.

"What of this so called Enterprise of England?" Henry Campernowne was saying. "Think you it has a chance of being successful?"

I strained to hear the answer, but either

Conn Galliard was more discreet than my uncle or he was further from the door.

"Well," continued my uncle after a while, "if as you say all the Catholic Princes are eager for Mary Stuart to sit on the throne, then it must have a better chance than the other mismanaged plots that have come to naught."

Again there was a pause, only an unintelligable murmur carrying to me and then my uncle spoke again, so near the door that I jumped.

"We expect him tomorrow," he said. "You'll stay and take part?"

Footsteps approached the door and without waiting for the answer, I picked up my skirts and fled, reaching my room out of breath and trembling with agitation. Scrambling out of my clothes, I flung myself into bed, not feeling safe until I lay under the coverings and could feign sleep if anyone opened my door.

Sleep was very hard to find that night. I lay awake and worried far into the small hours as I puzzled over my kinsman's words. How could he have heard of the Enterprise of England, I wondered when Sir Robert Varley seemed to think it was a secret matter, known only to the Queen's secret service and the people who had perpetrated it?

Try how I would, I could come to only one conclusion and biting my thumb, I admitted that my uncle must be a Catholic . . . not one who wished to worship quietly in his own way, but a man who was active in the cause and wanted a Queen of his own convictions on the throne of England, and for that he was prepared to act treasonably.

My blood ran cold at the thought and even though it was midsummer, I shivered like one with the chills, as I recalled my father's tales of the religious persecutions that had taken place during Mary Tudor's reign. When at last I fell asleep, my dreams were peopled with hideous figures in black masks wielding axes and instruments of torture, while their victims shrieked and cried for mercy.

I awoke, tired and drenched in perspiration, surprised to look out of the window and find the world so ordinary and normal seeming. Rising, I washed in cool water, wondering how I could act naturally towards my relations, knowing what I did . . . with a sudden flash of fear that sent a shiver dancing down my back, I realized my own danger if they should find out that I suspected their secret.

It was not until Mary was lacing my bodice that I recalled the visitor my uncle expected the next day and remembering the various strangers I had come upon before, determined to keep a watch for any faces that were not familiar to me. Settling the little ornate mirror on its chain about my waist, I lifted my chin and arranging as normal an expression as I could manage upon my face, I went down to breakfast.

3

TO my relief only Jane was at the breakfast table. My uncle was busy with his accounts, his wife could be heard berating some poor serving wench in the kitchens, and of Sir Conn there was no sign, Dudley having borne him off to look for sport in the hunting field.

All that day I wandered restlessly about Hawks' Hill, now in the house, now walking in the garden and courtyard, but try as I would, I could see no-one who in any way resembled a spy in the pay of the Spaniards. The only newcomer was a welcome pedlar, who arrived mid-morning astride a donkey who carried his master's wares in two basket panniers. I will confess I eyed him with suspicion as he rode in so conveniently, but one look at his bent back and aged countenance convinced me he was incapable of any lively action, treasonous or otherwise.

Jane and I spent a pleasurable time

selecting ribbons and thread from his pack, whilst my uncle seemed more interested in the news sheet the pedlar had brought with him, his brow growing darker and more thunderous with each word he read.

"Bad news, Uncle?" I enquired at last, curiosity overcoming my caution.

Glowering at me, he snorted through his nose and impatiently crumpled the paper in his hand, ignoring my question, and flung it in the direction of the fireplace. He then stalked out of the room.

Pouncing on it as soon as he had gone, I smoothed out the paper and began to read the thick, smudged print. I found I was reading a copy of a bill that had been read by town cryers at every market place in England. Suddenly my uncle's rage was clear; by law all Jesuit priests and all who helped them were to be accounted traitors! Of course everyone knew that priests from the Jesuit college at Douai were about their work in England, holding Mass in any house that wished for their services, but now their mission and their hosts would be in extreme danger. Whereas before, people who refused to attend the new Church of England had been tolerated and occasionally fined for their absence, now they would be prosecuted and perhaps even sent to prison or executed for their fault.

Suddenly the bright summer world seemed a dangerous place and as the paper slid from my nerveless fingers, I wished desperately that I was safe at home in Somerset again, secure with my gentle, scholarly father who was more interested in the ancient gods of the Greeks and Romans than any modern day religion.

Later that day, some time after the midday meal, I could bear the confines of the house no longer and braving the heat of the sun, took a shady straw hat and went into the garden.

Henry Campernowne had spared no expense in creating the surroundings to his new house. Clipped hedges bordered broad walks, smooth green lawns were edged with bright flower beds and here and there, where the whim had taken him, evergreens were trimmed into fanciful shapes. Of course, the topiaries were still small, but obviously my uncle had planned with an eye to the future; he was clearly sure that his descendants would enjoy the fruits of his labour.

I wandered slowly down one wide path and turned the corner. There, as though he had planned the encounter, Sir Conn waited, leaning elegantly against the stone sundial that marked the centre of the small green square, hedged about with privet.

Surprised, I involuntarily drew back and he raised one thin black eyebrow in amused query, not unfolding his arms or bowing to me as was expected between a lady and a gentleman.

Dropping into a formal curtsey to remind him of his manners, I remarked coldly that I would not disturb him and made to leave.

"I hope you are rested after your late night."

His words gave me pause and I turned slowly to face him. His tone was normal enough, even slightly amused, but with my recently acquired knowledge I had grown wary, half suspecting danger where none could be.

"Late, sir?" I queried, raising my eyebrows in turn. "You must know I left for my chamber before my aunt and cousin."

"Maybe," he answered unperturbed, "but I'd lay wager that you reached it well after they were asleep."

He came closer, by his stature making me look up to face him, and I saw that the eyes which I had thought blue, appeared grey in the sunlight.

"Mistress Perditta, the grass had been scythed yesterday, you brought it in on your shoes and left sign of your passage outside your uncle's room and all the way to your chamber."

I eyed him steadily. "I had need of the cooling air," I said calmly, "and took a turn about the garden."

He shook his head and told me I was foolish.

"How so?" I asked flatly.

"Have you not heard that the night air can be dangerous?" he asked. "I have known many maids like yourself struck down in their youth by wandering abroad when they should be safe abed."

"Rubbish!" I exclaimed, impatiently, "I had not suspected you to be a believer in old wives' tales. I daresay that the air of a town might be injurious to health, but in the country there can be no danger whatever."

"Take my word, mistress," he said seriously, "and shun the night air."

I fell silent, wondering at his tone, thinking he must be either teasing or flirting. Yet there was an underlying note of warning that I could not ignore and suddenly the warmth was gone from the sun and I shivered, feeling goosepimples break out on my skin.

"I am flattered at your care for me," I told my companion, "but I have guardians enough to watch over me . . . and am past the age that takes kindly to advice, however well meant."

He smiled. "Master Campernowne told me that your father had allowed you free rein."

"My father was the best of parents," I said quickly. "It ill behoves my uncle to disparage him."

"You must admit that he was a

little unusual in his attitude to his daughter — "

"If by that you mean that I was not taught to be meek and bow my head when a man was near, you are right. My father believed that men and women were equal. That my brain was no less because it was female. He educated me as he would have a son and taught me to have pride in myself as a person, regardless of my sex."

I faced Sir Conn proudly, meeting his eyes steadily, reading interest and speculation in their depths, before he deliberately concealed his thoughts.

"Sweetheart," he laughed, "I can see why Henry Campernowne is afraid of you. He likes to be the master in his house and I can clearly see that you will be a challenge to his leadership."

"And you?" I found myself asking outrageously.

His eyes narrowed, all laughter leaving them. "I enjoy a fight," he said, "but be warned, mistress, I don't fight fairly. I mean to win."

Looking into his eyes, I knew he meant his unequivocal statement. "N-no honour?" I wondered, breathlessly, "No gentlemanly honour?"

"None," he answered and I believed him. "In a fight I consider such an appendage totally useless."

Eyes wide, I stared at him. "Then let us hope we never have to do battle," I replied in a voice that shook, despite my efforts.

His eyes lit and he smiled, showing his teeth in his brown face. "What a fight that would be," he said loudly. "We'd wake the gods in their celestial beds! In truth, sweetheart, you'd find a worthy opponent in Conn Galliard."

"You overestimate yourself, Sir Boaster," I told him coldly and turned away.

Still laughing, he let me go and I was not sure if I was chagrined or no at his churlishness. The encounter had exhilarated me and something else . . . I sought to analyse my feelings and decided somewhat to my dismay that Sir Conn Galliard aroused something very akin to fear in me, but mixed with this emotion was a keen sense of anticipation, almost excitement. I read a ruthlessness in his manner, an arrogance and ready contempt for lesser mortals in his attitude, and while it attracted something akin in my nature — it repelled and frightened me. Sir Conn, I knew, was a dangerous man, with a power to attract me that made me feel like the moth that against all sense, flies into the flame of a candle.

Determined to prove my indifference, I pleaded a headache and forgoing dinner and its unwelcome company, stayed safe in my room, comforting myself that my uncle's house guest must soon leave and Hawks' Hill return to its usual uneventful existence, but Jane soon put such suppositions to flight.

"Oh, no," she answered to my question, when she came to my chamber bearing one of her mother's herb tisanes. "Sir Conn owns a house a few miles away. It has become badly in need of repair in his absence and he will stay here while the men are working on it."

"Oh, Jane," I cried, "how I wish he'd go!"

She looked at me in surprise. "I'll own that he is rather large and has a stern appearance and is not at all the kind of man I care for, but why are you so upset? He — has not forced himself upon you?"

I quickly put her mind at rest upon that score, but was at a loss to explain the cause of my nervousness. "I — he makes me feel like a mouse, while he is the cat eyeing what he sees as a tasty morsel."

Jane eyed me reflectively, a puzzled frown between her brows. "I've never thought of him in that way," she said. "He always seems polite."

"But he has an air about him," I protested. "I am sure he is quite ruthless — he would let no-one get in his way. He frightens me," I confessed.

"I am sure you are mistaken," my cousin said, mildly. "I expect it's the headache making you feel as you do. Drink mother's brew and perhaps you'll feel better. This hot weather agrees with none of us. I'm sure I feel bad tempered and ready to box someone's ear myself."

I had to smile at the thought of such an action on the part of my gentle cousin and what surprise and consternation it would arouse in the household. I expected her to stay and talk for a while, but she appeared restless, wandering around the room setting things to rights. At last she made an excuse and took herself off.

The first thing I did as soon as she was gone, was to empty Aunt Campernowne's tisane out of the window. In all things my aunt was thorough, and while I had no doubts as to the effectiveness of her work, I had found that the cure was generally worse than the illness. I half suspected her of inducing the dreadful taste deliberately on the principle that, knowing the vile physic that awaited them, her household would be less likely to admit to feeling unwell.

I sat at the open window enjoying the peaceful evening and the sweet scents from the garden while the family dined, but had returned to bed before I heard them dispersing. Soon the house fell quiet, an owl hooted as he searched the garden for his prey and I was awakened out of a light sleep by an unexpected sound.

Lifting my head from the pillow I listened, my ears straining. Just as I was on the point of relaxing it came again and I frowned in puzzlement. Music! Softly and quietly but, now that my ears were attuned, quite clearly the sound of people singing carried to me.

For a moment I sat upright in the high bed before flinging back the bedclothes. I slid my feet into slippers and wrapping a brocade nightgown around me for modesty, opened my bedroom door and peered out. The corridor was empty and dark save for the moon creeping in at the long mullioned window. Hesitating, I buttoned my nightgown before closing the door softly behind me, then I set off in the direction of the music.

The singing led me towards the attic, where I presumed the servants slept and where I had never been before. Pausing on my way as I came to Jane's room, I tapped and opening the door, peered in. To my amazement it was empty, her bed smock lying ready for use on the bed, but no sign of its owner.

With growing unease I continued along the passage, coming to a flight of stairs which I knew led to the attic. With one foot on the first step I raised my head and listened. From above me came the murmur of voices, not talking normally, but seeming to chant in unison and as I stared I could make out a faint light that edged the door at the top of the stairs.

Realizing that it was slightly ajar and overcome by curiosity, I hastened up the stairs and applied my eye to the crack only to find that I could see nothing of the room beyond. Disappointed, but determined not to be outdone, I gave the door a cautious push and at once a pewter plate which had been balanced above fell to the floor with a resounding crash. Before I could recover my wits the door flew open, a hand reached out and I was dragged roughly inside.

For a moment I stood blinking and gasping and then my eyes took in the scene before me. The low room was lit by candles and at the far end was what could only be an altar, while in front of it in the vestments of a priest stood a man whom I recognized with amazement as the pedlar. Between him and myself stood the members of the Campernowne household and various neighbours whom I recognized as having met that summer, in attitudes that bespoke surprise, fright and, in my uncle's case, anger.

For what seemed an age we stared at each other; then, becoming aware of the fingers that gripped my arm, I turned to see who held me captive. As I had half suspected it was Conn Galliard. Cold grey eyes stared down at me with a gaze that was far from kindly and for the first time a thrill of fear went through me.

"Oh, Perditta," wailed my cousin Jane. "Why didn't you drink the tisane?" and I realized with a sense of shock that the beverage must have been drugged.

The priest whispered in my uncle's ear and at his nod, spoke a blessing and his congregation began to disperse, until only himself, Sir Conn and my kinsmen were left in the room with me.

"Well, niece, you've been very foolish," said my uncle, unpleasantly, his face flushed and ugly with rage.

I shrugged myself free of Sir Conn's grasp and faced them calmly. "Why should it matter if I know you are recusants and hold Masses?" I asked. "I am no religious bigot — your faith is your own affair as far as I am concerned."

"But unfortunately not as far as anyone

else. You know a secret which could ruin me — all of us — and that is a state of affairs which I find insufferable."

"This is an affair for you to settle, husband," put in his wife, meaningly. "Pray, let Jane and me retire and leave you to your business."

With her hand on her daughter's arm, she sailed from the room. I tried to catch my cousin's eye as she passed, but she kept her gaze steadily downcast, refusing to look at me and I wondered miserably if I had lost my only friend at Hawks' Hill.

With their going, the atmosphere seemed to become even more tense and I eyed the other occupants of the room uneasily, while they regarded me coldly, speaking among themselves as if I could not hear.

"I am afraid she is a danger to the whole community," said the pedlar-priest, in accents far distant to those I had heard him use before. "She could identify all of us."

"I'll not have a danger in my household," agreed my uncle, watching as the priest put his vestments and vessels into a leather box and then hid them under the floorboards.

Something in the complete lack of secrecy filled me with unease, he seemed to feel that there was no need to hide his actions from me, as though my knowing their whereabouts was of little import.

The men fell silent, turning to eye me speculatively. Their cold gaze filling me with alarm, but determined not to show my fear I lifted my chin and returned their glance with as much calm as I was able to summon.

"Well, niece," said my uncle, with a show of unexpected affability, "no need to look about to swoon. I'll take you back to your chamber and a tisane brewed by my wife will soon calm you and give you a good night."

I started back at his approach and in an instant Sir Conn was between me and the door. "Think you I am some numbskull that I don't know you intend to put some potion in it that would ensure so deep a sleep that I'd never waken again?"

Master Campernowne halted, watching me with small furious eyes. "You'll take it willingly or by force," he said harshly.

"I'll fight," I warned, backing away. "I'll make such a rumpus — "

My uncle laughed, throwing back his head on his short neck. "We're all of the old religion here," he told me. "Do you think I'd choose any save those of my own faith to serve me? Shout as much as you like — little good it will do you. To tell the truth I'd enjoy a fight with you, wench. Many's the time I've felt the wish to beat you since you came to my house."

I was against the wall now and knew that with another stride my uncle would seize me. Already his thick red hands were reaching out for me and in desperation I tried a plea to his sense of family.

"I'm your kinswoman — your sister's child. Doesn't our relationship mean anything to you?"

My uncle stood looking down at me, his face growing alarmingly congested with rage. He blew through his nose, making an ugly sound, expressive of derision. "Kinswoman!" he snorted. "*You!*" His tiny eyes ran over me, withering in their contempt and dislike. "My sister was well past the age of bearing children when you were foisted on her. You must have been a byblow of scholarly Master John Fox's or some gypsy's brat. Whoever you are, I do know, you're no Campernowne. With your red hair you're nothing like any of us. You, Mistress Perditta, are some nameless bastard and I owe you no act of relationship."

I stared at him blankly, almost unable to accept his unbelievable statement, but from the depths of my memory odd incidents and memories thought forgot and brought to mind by his words, arose to confound me. There had been times when I had looked at myself in the mirror and wondered at the dissimilarities between my parents and myself. There *had* been conversations half heard and quickly smothered that had puzzled me at the time . . . and there was the odd matter of the five thousand pounds left to me by my penniless father.

A rough grasp on my hand brought me back to the present and bending my head I sank my teeth into my uncle's thick wrist. With a cry of pain he released me and I ran to the door, forgetting that Conn Galliard stood guard there, until I found myself imprisoned in his arms. Maddened by fear and my uncle's words, I fought for freedom, using teeth and nails and every weapon God had given me. Sir Conn laughed and used his strength on me until I was bruised and breathless and limp in his grasp.

"Give her to me," commanded my uncle. "I'll take her below and deal with her."

"Hold hard, Master Campernowne," said the man who held me. "I believe you run on a trifle too quickly."

"How so?" demanded the older man belligerently, not used to having his orders questioned.

Sir Conn loosened his grip on me a little and I could breath again. "Methinks that I have heard this Mistress Perditta has a Royal Godmother . . . I have also heard that that lady takes great interest in her Godchildren. If one of those was to disappear unexpectedly, might she not cause inconvenient enquires to be made?"

"Rubbish!" exclaimed my uncle, making an impatient gesture. "Females die all the time. She had a headache this very evening — a sudden fever that carried her off despite my wife's ministries. It's all the excuse needed."

"I think we should consider the matter," put in the priest's quiet voice. "What had you in mind, Sir Conn?"

"I believe that a wife may not testify against her husband."

"That is so," agreed the other thoughtfully.

"Then nothing would be simpler than to wed her to someone on whom we can rely."

"Of course, Dudley is most suitable — " began my uncle quickly. "And I could keep her under my eye."

"The boy's too young for such responsibility," said Sir Conn easily. "Someone older and more able to control her is required. Gentlemen, I offer myself — moreover I would point out that I have the advantage of a house some miles distant, well away from passing traffic and more inaccessible."

Angry at the thought of losing my money, my uncle blustered, but was overruled by the quiet priest, while Dudley mewed ineffectually.

"The Queen will not allow it," I

protested, twisting my head to glare up at my captor.

"It's that — or death," he answered grimly and looking at the dark figures of the other men, as the candles flared and their shadows danced across the walls, I knew he spoke the truth and shivered and fell silent.

"If we are all agreed, I would have the ceremony performed now. That way there can be no — mistake." The voice above my head spoke to the other men, clearly expecting to be obeyed, and no-one thought to question his command.

Quickly the priest was vested in his embroidered garments again and almost before I was aware of what was happening, Sir Conn and I were standing side by side while he read the marriage service over us. Sir Conn took a heavy gold ring from his little finger and slipped it over mine at the appropriate moment. I would have refused when the priest asked if I was willing, but one look at the face above me and the hard, closed face of my uncle and I knew that I had no choice. Comforting myself with the thought that the wedding was not lawful, I remained quiet and acquiescent, starting a little when the man beside me demanded his marriage lines.

Without a word the priest took paper and quill and for a few moments the scratching of his pen filled the room as he wrote busily. Having read what he had written, Sir Conn folded the document and thrust it into his doublet, turning to me as he refastened the tiny gold buttons.

"Let me take you back to your chamber," he said courteously, and for a moment I wondered if I had dreamed all that had passed, but his next words dispelled any such notion. "We'll start for Galliard's Hay early in the morning, so get as much rest as you can."

Docilely I allowed him to lead me downstairs, even returning his bow as I entered my room. The lock turned behind me and as though in a dream, I walked to the bed and sinking down, stared blankly ahead of me. So much had happened in the last hour that I found it hard to believe, only the sharp pain as I pinched my wrist assuring me that I was not asleep. Within the space of a short while I had had aspersions cast on my parentage and married a man, a stranger of whom I knew nothing, save that he was a Catholic and wealthy. That he was an adventurer and ruthless were suspicions rather than facts; nevertheless, I believed them true and grew chill at the thought of sharing my life with such a man.

At that moment I heard the key turning cautiously in the lock and watched as a slip of paper was pushed under the door. Approaching it carefully, half suspecting some new trick, I touched it with the toe of my slipper before bending down and picking it up.

One line of hasty writing was scrawled across its surface and reading it, I felt hope renewing itself. "A horse is saddled," was all it said, but I knew that a way of escape had been presented to me and hastily began to dress.

Wrapping a dark cloak around me, I paused, one hand on the door, sorry to leave all my clothes behind. Seeing the note gleaming white on the floor where I had dropped it, I quickly thrust it under my skirt into my pocket, knowing the trouble that would face Jane if it was found and my uncle realized that she had helped me.

The house was dark and quiet and, mindful of the need for caution, I flitted like a ghost to a side door, finding the bolts already drawn back. The cold night air took my breath away, turning me sick and faint with reaction, and I leaned against the rough brick wall for a few seconds before I could gather enough strength in my trembling knees to run to the stable.

The horses greeted me with soft, surprised neighs, and I had to spend a few minutes calming them before I was able to lead out the one already saddled. As I walked him along the grass verge of the drive, the sky lightened and looking up I saw that dawn was not far distant. Judging myself far enough away from Hawks' Hill, I pulled myself into the saddle and cantered to the road where I paused, uncertain of the way to choose. Making up my mind, I turned the horse towards London and putting him into a gallop, soon left my uncle's house behind.

4

RIDING into the early morning mist, past the fields and hedges thick with dew, I suddenly realized that for all the heat of the weather, the summer was gone and it being October, the devil had already touched the blackberries that clustered on the bramble bushes bordering the road.

When I judged I was safe from pursuit, I reined in my mount — for I wished to save him for the long journey ahead — and reviewed my hastily formed plans. The Queen had forbade me the Court, but once in London I could send a message to Sir Robert Varley and surely she would not refuse me help in such circumstances. Luckily I had had the forethought to slip her pearls about my neck and so would not be penniless. Feeling suddenly free and careless, I kicked my heels into my horse, startling him out of the gentle amble into which he had fallen as my attention wandered and with a little spurt of speed rounded a corner of the road.

On the verge, hidden until then by a gorse bush, a horseman waited, one hand on his hip, his whole attitude bespeaking a cheerful content with the world.

"I bid you goodmorrow, sweetheart," cried Sir Conn, as though we had arranged to meet at that particular place.

After one horrified glance, I recovered my senses and jabbed my heels into my mount's sides, urging him forward in a desperate endeavour to escape. In a second, Con Galliard's black stallion was barring the way, making my little mare neigh and rear with fright. A brown hand seized my rein and wild with fear and anger, I struck out blindly with my riding crop at the dark figure. Heedless of my blows, he brought my horse under control, leaning out of his saddle to bring the flying hooves firmly to the ground. Only then did he turn his head to look at me and I gasped a little at the livid red weal that crossed his cheek.

"Have a care, mistress," he warned quite gently, but something in his eyes made me relinquish the switch without a fight as he wrenched it from my hand and snapping it in two, threw it contemptuously aside.

"And now," he went on with a smile I did not like, "we'll continue our journey."

"Where are you taking me?" I asked as we moved off.

"To Galliard's Hay — where else?"

I digested this for a while as we rode on in silence. "How did you know where to find me?" I asked at last.

"It wasn't hard to fathom out that you'd seek the shelter of the Queen — after that," he shrugged broad shoulders eloquently, "it was easy. I spent my boyhood in this area. I know all the paths and shortcuts." He looked down at me curiously. "Was it true — what your uncle said about your parentage?"

"I don't know," I answered crossly. "Does it matter to anyone but me?"

"It might. I daresay it does to your real parents. Have you any idea where they are?"

"I had not suspected anything of the kind until my uncle made his suspicions clear." Even to myself my voice sounded hesitant and uncertain. "That's not quite true," I found myself saying, to my surprise. "There *have* been one or two little things, now that I look back. Nothing much, just an unwillingness to talk about certain things — where I was born. Women usually talk about their confinements, my mother didn't."

"I see."

We rode on but my companion seemed unwilling to let the subject drop. "Your mother, she was a Campernowne?" he asked.

"Yes, she was cousin to Katherine Ashley, who was a Campernowne before she married and who was governess to the Queen. My father was friends with her husband, John Ashley, who was Keeper of the Jewel House."

He seemed amused. "You have grand connections."

"Not now," I answered soberly. "My Aunt Kate died when I was a little girl."

"You were fond of her?"

"I did not see her often," I told him truthfully, "but when I did, I recall she was kind." Suddenly I remembered to whom I was talking so freely and drew my reservation around me. "The Queen will not let me wed you," I said coldly. "She has already refused consent to one Catholic."

"Perhaps these circumstances will persuade her."

"What do you mean?"

"I mean sweetheart, that she will hardly refuse permission if we are already living together as man and wife." Seeing my expression, he laughed and urged our mounts to greater speed.

"She'll send you to the Tower," I cried furiously. "You wouldn't dare!"

"I would," he said. "Oh, I would," and rode on whistling.

We came upon Galliard's Hay some time before noon. Splendidly placed in thickly wooded countryside, it stood at the top of a steep ravine like road, commanding a view to the distant hills that bounded the horizon. The house itself was old, made of flint and wood and stood foresquare and solid, mullioned, oriel windows protruding from its thick walls. I found its appearance to my liking, its air of permanence reminding me of my home in Somerset. Even with piles of wooden planks and heaps of rubbish lying outside, giving evidence of the work being done, the house still had an air of welcome about it.

The man beside me sighed, a sound of pleasure and content and I looked up startled that such a person should feel so simple an emotion; I had supposed Conn Galliard to care more for the rich, impressive and adventurous things of life.

Catching my gaze, he smiled, for once his expression neither alight with sardonic amusement nor the remote shrewdness I had come to expect. "Welcome home," he said.

"Why has it such a curious name?" I asked as we rode forward.

"My father used to say that King Henry named it so when he stayed here. It had so many rooms and passages that he said it reminded him of the dance called a Hay. However that is just a conceit, for it is called Priest's Hay in old documents — I believe hay is an ancient word for an enclosure."

"It's certainly very old," I agreed, eyeing the flint walls and ancient timbers. Even the doorstep was worn and rounded where many feet had passed over it.

"It belonged to the priests of Winchester, until they grew poor with the Reformation and my father bought it."

Tossing the reins of his horse to a boy who had come running at his shout, he came to help me dismount and looking down into his eyes as he held up his arms, I hesitated before trusting myself to him.

"Come down, sweetheart," he laughed. "You can't sit there forever!"

Reluctantly I slid into his arms, feeling his hands tight about my waist as I rested my hands on his shoulders. For a breathless moment he held me, my feet clear of the ground, before he let me slide slowly down his body.

To hide my confusion, I quickly stepped into the house, narrowly avoiding being hit by a length of wood that a small man was carrying over one shoulder, his heavy apron and sacking bag of tools proclaiming his calling.

"The head carpenter," explained Sir

Conn as the other man bowed. "Little John is worth two men twice his size. He works like a Trojan."

"I shall be interested to see his work," I said, gravely.

A glance passed between the two men — inquiring on the carpenter's part and undoubtedly warning on Sir Conn's. Little John nodded and walked away, while I followed his retreating figure with interest; so, here was another who was not all he seemed, I thought, and wondered if the little man was a Papist priest.

I turned to find Conn Galliard watching me with lazy amusement in his eyes and saw by his expression that he had read my thoughts.

"Well, Sir," I said, quickly, "if I am to housekeep here, I must look over my domain. Show me around your property."

Most of the servants were taking advantage of their master's absence and were about their own business. The cook, having taken the opportunity to sample the wine cellar was asleep in the kitchen and when I explored the house, I found the rooms either in the process of being restored or damp and cobweb-laden. Only the chamber beyond the entrance hall was habitable and here new panelling smelled sweetly and once a fire was lit in the huge fireplace it began to assume a hospitable air.

A table and two chairs were dragged in and fresh straw from the stables spread over the floor, while the cook roused himself enough to prepare a meal. Sir Conn had taken himself off, leaving me to my own devices, and once I had set the remaining servants about their business, I gave my attention to the house.

The central core was a massive stone chimney, built when the old great hall was divided into two and now serving both the entrance hall and the smaller room beyond. The fireplace in the hall was large and ornately carved, its aged stone appearing old and dark against the new panels which were being fitted to the lath and plaster walls. I was interested to see that a new cupboard had been fitted into the side of the stone chimney and stepped closer to open the door and peer inside.

"I hope you approve of my work, mistress," said a voice behind me, startling me with its unexpectedness.

"It seems of the highest order," I told Little John, who seemed to be able to move with little sound. "But placing a cupboard in the hall seems a little unusual."

"I believe Sir Conn wishes to keep wine there — for visitors. Will it inconvenience you if I get on with my work? Now that you are in residence, Sir Conn wants us to hurry our pace."

Without waiting for my permission, he took up a hammer and drove me from the hall with a positive volley of blows that echoed about the empty room and made my head ring with the clamour.

"Has the carpenter a surname?" I asked Sir Conn that evening as we sat over our wine and cheese, the only passable part of the meal the cook had sent in to us.

He did not look up. "I've never heard it," he answered briefly.

"He doesn't speak like a workman," I

went on. "I wonder why he undertakes so menial a job."

"Perhaps he likes it." There was a warning note in his voice and I looked up to meet his eyes across the table. "Leave it, Perditta — your curiosity has already got you into trouble."

"So he is a renegade of some kind . . . a priest or a Catholic agent."

Sir Conn sighed. "As far as I know the fellow is a workman going about his legitimate business. He handles a chisel and saw too well to be a priest, I'd say, but imagine what you like, sweetheart." He seemed indifferent about the matter, yawning and stretching his arms wide. "Faith, but I'm tired," he said. "Let's go to bed," and smiled when he saw the consternation on my face.

"All the beds are damp," I said, deliberately trying to conceal my agitation. "The mattresses smell of mildew and are no doubt filled with mice . . . certainly not fit for humans to use."

"We'll be comfortable here with the straw for a bed and my cloak for covering." Leaving his seat, he came to my side of the table, pushing aside the used plates to perch on the edge, one long leg swinging. "Look at me, sweetheart," he said, tugging gently at the strings that tied my ruff.

When I made no move his brown fingers took my chin and turned it up. The fire had died away, the only candles we had found gave little light and in the shadows it was hard to read his expression. Suddenly he released my chin and taking both my hands in his, carried them to his lips.

I shivered a little; all day I had refused to contemplate this encounter, which I knew must take place. Most marriages were arranged, but in this case I had had no say at all in the matter. Even in the dark room I could read implacability in the posture of the man before me and knew that he was very sure of winning his objective.

Gently he drew me to my feet, my hands still imprisoned in his. His beard brushed my cheek and then his mouth found mine. A shiver that was not all fear, but possessed something of both excitement and anticipation, shook me.

"Seduction, not anything more forceful,

is my aim," he breathed against my ear. "You didn't think otherwise?"

Much later, I lay watching the red embers of the fire fall into ash. "She'll send you to the Tower, you know," I remarked conversationally.

"Not if you petition her sweetly enough," Sir Conn answered comfortably, drawing me on to his shoulder.

Warm and relaxed, I lay examining his face in the dim glow from the dying fire. He had been a kind and considerate lover and while I knew that there was no love between us, many marriages had started out under worse circumstances. Given good fortune, I felt that Conn Galliard and I could make a future together that would be better than I had anticipated a short while ago. Determined to write to the Queen the next day I fell asleep and awoke to find the morning far advanced and my husband gone from my side.

Having made what toilet I could, I breakfasted before making a housewifely round and finally went in search of Sir Conn.

"C-Conn," I said, his name coming strangely to my lips.

"Perditta." He turned and spoke my name in much the same tone I had used. His face was grave but something in the back of his eyes, a certain knowledge as his gaze travelled over me, made me blush and stammer in confusion.

"I — was looking for paper and a pen," I said breathlessly. "Pray, tell me where they are to be found and I will write to the Queen . . ." His expression had changed and my voice died away uncertainly. "I thought that was what you wanted," I faltered.

"I do — but there is no need for hurry. We'll wait a while yet and be more certain of her answer."

"What do you mean?" I asked, puzzled.

"I think your education was lacking in some vital details. Sweetheart, if we can say you are with child, her Majesty will be the more like to give her consent."

I stared at him, rage growing in me. "You would use me like a brood mare!" I told him angrily and seeing the bawdy reply spring to his lips, ran from him determined to find the paper and ink that I was sure must be tucked away in some corner of that vast house.

Search how I would, I could find none and had to admit defeat until I thought of the steward's account book that lay forgotten in the little chamber next to the huge kitchen. To my disappointment, the book was out of date and seemed full of spiky, angular writing and figures, and I was ready to cry with frustration until I found a page that was only half covered in accounts. Ripping it out with shaking fingers, I tore off the top half and found myself left with a reasonably sized piece of paper.

Soot and water made a passable ink and I had already noticed a dusty goose feather lying forgotten in the corner of the room. Sharpening the quill proved difficult, it being a task that my father had always taken upon himself, but at the cost of a bloody finger, I managed it at last, and, brushing aside debris and accumulated rubbish, I sat down at the desk to write my letter.

Selecting Sir Robert as being the more likely to come to my rescue, I set out my sad circumstances and begged for his aid in tones calculated to wring his heart and spur his manly pride into acting like a knight of romance.

I was just setting my name to it, when a brown hand came over my shoulder and carried it off. Turning in rage and panic, I saw Sir Conn give it a cursory glance, before crumpling it into a ball and tossing it contemptuously into a far corner, his eyes cold as ice and furiously angry.

With fingers crooked, I flew at him, leaving a row of bloody scratches before he could catch my hands and hold me prisoner before him. Gradually his grip tightened until I gave up my struggles for freedom, warned that pain was not far away.

"Y-you are hurting me," I said and was annoyed to find that my voice shook.

"I should beat you," he said almost conversationally.

I made no answer, knowing that if he should decide upon such an action there was very little I could do about it. Lifting my head I faced him squarely, meeting his eyes with as steady a gaze as I could muster, hoping he would not read the fear I felt. His grip on my wrists tightened until I bit my lip to keep from whimpering and then I was suddenly free as he flung me away from him and strode towards the door.

"I realize that no ties of affection bind us," I hurled at his departing back, "but as your wife my honour must be of some import to you."

He turned in the open doorway, one hand on the latch and looked me over coldly. "You will petition the Queen when you carry my child and not before," he said implacably and slammed the door closed behind him.

Over the next few days the anger between us gradually dissolved until we had returned to our former wary relationship. Mary and a wagon bearing my clothes had arrived from Hawks' Hill and the servants and the steward having returned, I threw myself into an orgy of housework, setting the maids to sewing curtains for the rooms that Master Little John and his men were renovating with considerable success. Soon the old house seemed to take on a new lease on life, growing warm and comfortable under my guidance and I could look at my handiwork with a glow of pride in my achievement.

* * *

Looking out of the window one morning, I saw the countryside covered in a thick, white frost and realized that winter had come unnoticed while I was busy with the house.

"What month is it?" I asked Sir Conn who, having come in from visiting an outlying farm, bringing a cloud of cold air with him, was warming his hands at the logs burning in the grate.

"November," he answered idly, his mind still on business matters.

"You'd best let me have paper and pen — I have need to write a letter."

For a moment he continued to stretch his hands to the blaze, then my words sank in and he turned his head to stare at me.

"You mean — ?"

I nodded. "You've done your work well," I told him, "now make an honest woman of me."

He was across the room and had

97

gathered me close, but not before I had seen the expression on his face.

"You're pleased?" I asked needlessly, as I lay against his chest, the wild beating of his heart sounding in my ear.

"Give me a son, sweetheart," he said, "and I'll give you the world."

I was to remember his words later, but at that moment I was content with his fervour and obvious pleasure in my news. And so the next few days were spent in bitter struggle with quill and paper. Never having written to a queen before I found the task difficult, the formal phrases coming only with great effort to my pen. Having to plead and cajole and yet state my case in a way that would not anger her, made my head ache and covered my fingers with ink stains and the floor with discarded attempts.

At last one seemed better than the others and I was just reading it anew when my husband entered, pausing on the threshold to take in the state of the untidy room and my own distracted air. Wearily I held out the completed letter for his approval, rubbing my aching brow and for a moment I thought to read unaccustomed tenderness in his glance before he turned his attention to the paper.

"A masterpiece!" he declared. "It would wring a heart of stone. How thankful I am that your father didn't neglect your education."

"Who will take it?" I demanded.

"Someone reliable. I'll not have it lost or mislaid on the way."

"I'll take it myself."

Surprised, I turned to look at him and he met my gaze with a bland innocence which I found disturbing.

"I'll add my own plea," he said, adding with an air of indifference that as it was an age since he was in the capital, he had had a mind to visit London for some time. "I'll bring you stuff for a new gown," he promised and with that I had to be content, extracting only a promise for a length of velvet as I waved him farewell a few days later.

With Sir Conn's absence the house seemed strangely quiet and empty. Disliking my own company I went early to bed and was surprised to be woken some time later by the sounds of what could only be furtive carpentry. Knowing that Little John was on the point of finishing his work I was surprised by the need of anyone to be about so late and lay puzzling for a few minutes, before my curiosity overcame my caution and I pulled on a velvet nightgown to cover my shift and cautiously opened my chamber door. Mindful of the last time I had left my bed at night I was reluctant to venture out into the dark house, but reminding myself that I was mistress of Galliard's Hay and that none within its walls would dare harm me, I left the shelter of my room and crept silently to the head of the stairs.

The sounds came from below and kneeling on the cold wooden boards, I peered through the banister. At first I could see nothing while the muffled tapping went on and then a faint glow appeared beside the great stone fireplace, until the newly built cupboard was illuminated from within like a stage for a play.

Catching my breath I waited, half expecting a ghost or goblin to appear and it was almost with relief that I saw the figure of a real and solid man step out of the cupboard, reach above his head and pull down the shelves behind him. In the faint light from the lantern he carried, I recognised the sharp features of Little John and crouched lower as he lifted his lantern and stared upward, seeming to sense that he was being watched.

After an age, he appeared satisfied that he was alone and moving silently crossed the hall and left by a side door. Wondering what I had discovered, I ran to my room, determined to examine the cupboard at the first opportunity that presented itself.

Next morning, deciding to help opportunity along a little, I found a long and complicated job for Master John in the farthest stable and as soon as I was sure he had set to work, hurried to the great hall. Setting a stool against the door to the kitchens I had only the stairs to bother about and as the maids were busy in the bed-chambers and their own quarters, knew that the chances of being disturbed were very slight.

Even when I had taken out the wine flagons and goblets, the cupboard appeared innocent of any other purpose than that for which it had ostensibly been built. I was beginning to wonder if I had dreamed the previous night's adventure, when I recalled that the carpenter had reached up behind the front of the door and my searching fingers found a wooden latch. With its release, the whole of the back of the cupboard pivoted upward, revealing a gaping black void.

Feeling my hands shake with excitement, I lit a taper from the fire and holding it at arm's length peered into the opening. A small room, only a few feet square and obviously cut out from the stone chimney, met my gaze. The walls appeared neatly plastered and a bench against one wall was provided. Flagstones covered the floor and if a candle was provided I could see that it would be quite a snug retreat.

Thoughtfully I closed the entrance and blew out my taper, while I wondered for whom the secret room was intended. I had heard vaguely of such hideyholes in Catholic houses when they were called priest holes, but this was the first time I had been in close contact with one.

Knowing the measures taken against those hiding Jesuits, I grew cold with dread that my husband was obviously involved with the Papists. I knew too a little surprise that he was so involved; during our short marriage he seemed to have only a healthy regard for religion and while I knew he had been associated with my uncle, he appeared to have none of his hidden fanaticism.

Deciding to say nothing of my discovery, I waited for his return and a week or so later, felt a sudden sense of excitement as I heard horsemen approaching and flying to the window, saw a figure that could only be my husband's cantering towards the house. A man riding beside him seemed familiar and I only waited to make certain of his identity before sending the servants running about their business and hurrying myself to meet Sir Conn and his guest.

5

BY careful planning I managed to be at the bottom of the stairs as the steward opened the outer door and the men entered. Sinking into a graceful curtsey befitting the lady of a substantial house, I bid them welcome but my elegant effect was somewhat spoiled by my husband scooping me up in a bearhug and planting a noisy kiss on my mouth.

Setting my lace cap to rights I gave Sir Robert Varley my hand, smiling with genuine pleasure as he bowed over it, my heart fluttering strangely at his touch.

"A pleasant surprise," I told him. "I did not know you knew my husband."

"I came upon the Queen's business," he said gravely, while Sir Conn broke in to say that he had called upon him with my letter, when first in London.

Striding to the cupboard by the fire, he took out wine and glasses. Although I watched carefully I could not tell by his attitude whether he knew of the secret hiding place or not; certainly he treated it with scant respect, closing the door with a push of his shoulder as he turned back into the room.

"There's a bolt of cloth for you, Perditta," he said casually, "and a few other gewgaws to please you."

I was impatient to hear the outcome of his errand. "What news do you bring?" I demanded.

"News?" He pondered and turned to the other man for help. "What news do we bring Sir Robert? A new playhouse has opened on the South Bank, called the Rose Theatre after the inn nearby . . . Her Majesty has a curious new fan that folds into half its size . . . "

Mindful of the amused Sir Robert, I curbed the impulse to stamp my foot. "What of my petition?"

He pretended indifference and turned away. "You'd best ask Sir Robert," he said, pouring more wine.

I looked towards the Queen's man and he took pity on me, taking a rolled paper from his doublet and handing it to me with a bow. Two red ribbons dangled from its heavy wax seal but now that the Queen's answer lay in my hands, I regarded it hesitantly, strangely reluctant to open it and learn the fate of my unborn babe. Thinking that the news could not be totally bad as Sir Conn had returned to Galliard's Hay and not been lodged in the Tower, I slid my nail under the wax to break the seal and going to the window to make the most of the winter daylight, sank down upon the windowseat to read my letter.

Looking up I found both men watching me, Sir Conn's right eyebrow roused familiarly. "Well?" he asked.

"She says we have her blessing," I said, feeling stunned by the ease with which she had complied with my request. "She even sends me a Wedding present!"

The men seemed amused by my amazement, dragging me up and insisting that I drink a toast with them.

"We'd best set the day," said Sir Conn. "I'll make arrangements and ride over to invite your uncle and his family."

I looked at him quickly, but waited until we were alone before mentioning the matter again.

"I have no wish to see Henry Campernowne," I said, sitting up in bed, hugging my knees, while my husband toasted himself before the fire.

"I think it's time we let bygones be bygones," he remarked lazily.

"He would have murdered me," I reminded him, my voice bleak.

"Oh, surely not — I think you have forgotten the true events and dramatized those you remember."

I looked at him, feeling my eyes widen at his words. "Forgotten! How could I forget? You were there, you *know* he would have killed me but for you."

Sir Conn rose and shedding his dressing gown climbed into bed beside me. "Sweetheart," he said, taking me in his arms, "there are some things that it is best to let slip from your mind and this is one of them. I intend to invite the Camperownes here for Christmas."

I lay stiff and resentful. "I dislike him. How can I pretend otherwise?"

"You will do it, my love, because I ask it of you," he answered and fell to kissing my fingertips one by one.

"Why?" I questioned, not to be distracted.

"I am a peaceable man and would be friends with my neighbours," he told me.

One quick look at his face told me that he knew I did not believe him and did not care about my disbelief. Later though, I returned to the matter — one akin to it and something that had been puzzling me for some time.

"Why did you marry me, Conn?" I asked.

"God's Death! What a woman for questions!" he exclaimed. "I married you, Mistress Galliard, because I felt the need of a wife. I realized one day that unless I produced an heir, a distant kinsman, one that I dislike more than usual, will inherit all I own . . . and so when I came to Hawks' Hill I was looking out for a wife."

"I'm surprised that you didn't offer for Jane," I said, sourly.

Conn grinned suddenly. "You're more to my liking, sweetheart — besides you have the advantage of being an heiress and not possessing a tyrant for a father!"

I looked at him. "I had no idea that you had need of money," I said.

He leaned back against the pillows. "One always can find a use for wealth," he told me lazily. "And also friends, so we'll invite your kinsmen for the Christmas holiday and perhaps a few of the local gentry. The Deaths . . . Bess Death can be relied upon to enliven any gathering."

I pricked up my ears; this was the first time I had heard that lady's name mentioned, but by what seemed a coincidence I was to meet her within a few days. Conn and Sir Robert were out, seeking to fill the larder, when Mary came to me with the information that a lady was below asking for me. Half suspecting that Jane Campernowne had come in answer to one of the letters I had sent her, I hurried to the Great Hall, only to pause on the threshold at the sight of a complete stranger standing by the fire.

The tall, dark woman turned at my entrance, studying me with bold black eyes, making no effort to hide her interest.

Disliking her scrutiny, I lifted my

eyebrows and enquired coldly, "You wished to see me, madam? I think we have not met."

She came forward saying easily, "So you are Conn's new little wife." Her eyes travelled over me, her gaze amused and slightly derisive as though she was relieved for some reason at my appearance. "I am Bess Death," she went on, "and having heard tales of the new chatelaine at Galliard's Hay, felt the need to make your acquaintance,"

"I am honoured," I said.

She recognised the dry note in my voice, for her eyebrows shot up and her expression held a spark of anger. "When were you married, Lady Galliard?" she asked. "News travels so slowly in the country that we have had no knowledge of your wedding."

"We were married some months ago at my uncle's house," I said lightly, realizing my danger and her obvious suspicions.

Accepting my offer of refreshment, she sat down, for which I was grateful. Being of small stature myself I have no liking for peering up at another woman. Mistress Death was as tall and well built as an Amazon of old and feeling rather like a sparrow pecking around the feathers of a full grown blackbird, I gave her wine and cakes.

"Do you live nearby?" I asked, making conversation.

"A few miles away, near Alton. We have expected a visit from you and Sir Conn, but he's kept you so close that we began to suspect a love match."

Her tone was derisory and the sparkling glance she sent me so full of suppressed mirth that I felt my gorge rising.

"Sir Conn has been in London, receiving congratulations from my Godmother, the Queen," I said and had the satisfaction to see that my words had given her pause; however she recovered quickly and dipped her head in mock humility.

"I had no idea that your connections were so auspicious," she said. "I see I shall have to mind my manners when I come acalling. Master Death and I look forward to our visit at Christmas."

I looked at her in some surprise and a swift calculation told me that Conn must have issued his invitations before he mentioned it to me. Hiding my emotions I sipped from my glass. "My kinsmen from Hawks' Hill may come so we shall have a full house. A friend of mine, Sir Robert Varley, will be here as well."

"Will you keep the old traditions and choose a Lord of Misrule? I must confess to a liking for roisterous games — though my husband would rather sit by the fire and doze."

Her full, red lips pouted in mock dismay and I knew as she meant me to, that her husband's wishes had no effect upon his wife's behaviour.

"Master Death is . . . an older man?" I inquired delicately.

"He could be my grandfather." She lowered her eyelids and a small smile played across her mouth. "Being wife to an old man has its advantages. Before marriage one has to be so careful, but afterwards one need only be discreet!"

Shocked by her words, I made no attempt to hide my feelings. "I regard my marriage vows with respect," I told her severely.

"How virtuous," she laughed, "but I

am afraid that few men are as noble."

I was saved from making reply by the entrance of Sir Robert and my husband, both of whom to my disgust greeted my flamboyant visitor with enthusiasm and every sign of pleasure.

"I didn't know you knew Mistress Death," I said waspishly to my husband as soon as we were alone and I could voice my annoyance.

Sir Conn laughed. "Most of the county knows Bess Death," he answered, and I realized that he was fully aware of her views on morality.

"And yet you invite her here?"

"As I said, she can ensure the success of any gathering."

"A fine Christmas household you present me with — a woman with a reputation the whole county knows and a pack of my murderous kinsfolk!"

"I had not thought you a prude and I am well aware of your courage." His voice was quiet and his hands as he drew me to him were gentle. "What ails you, wife?" he asked. At his question my emotions overwhelmed me and somewhat to my surprise as well as his, I flung myself upon his chest and burst into floods of tears.

"I am not even married," I sobbed. "That — that *woman* was asking when we were wed. When the banns are called in Church, she and all Hampshire will know that you have ruined me. She'll *gloat* . . . and I c-can't bear it!"

Sir Conn presented me with a fine cambric handkerchief from his sleeve and then folded me in a comforting embrace. "Dear me," he said, mildly. "Such a do."

I bawled anew at his lack of sensibility and clenching my fists would have beaten upon his chest, but for the fact that his next words arrested me.

"What a good thing that the Queen is sending her own priest to officiate at a private ceremony."

"Can she arrange such things?" I wondered, raising a blotched and tear-stained face.

"After all she is the Head of the Church. He should arrive within the week. Upon my honour you'll be safely and lawfully wedded before Christmas."

He kept his word and I could face the

holy season with equinamity and loosen my stays with a clear conscience at the same time I set about preparing for our house guests. The month drew on and soon Galliard's Hay was filled with the warm, inviting smell of cooking and the sharp scent of holly and mistletoe. With growing enthusiasm, the cook undertook to surpass himself and as his cooking had lately improved beyond measure, apart from a few suggestions, I left him much to his own devices. Determined that no comfort should be found lacking and that no eye, however sharp, should be able to discern my housewifely fault, I set the maids to work to scour and polish, supervising myself the putting of hot bricks in the beds for days before the guests were expected, to be sure that no hint of dampness remained in the mattresses. At last, certain that no criticism could be applied, I relaxed, filled with a sense of pride at my handiwork, knowing that only praise could come my way.

I had pondered on my uncle's demeanour at our first meeting since I left Hawks' Hill so suddenly, but nothing had prepared me for his greeting when the Campernowne's arrived on Christmas Eve. Climbing heavily down from his horse, he would have embraced me, but for the fact that I quickly put out my hands, refusing his kiss as though I had not noticed his gesture. His touch filled me with revulsion and I turned away as quickly as possible to acknowledge Dudley and his mother and greet Jane more warmly.

"You didn't answer my letters," I whispered under cover of the general exchange behind us.

"Dear Perditta, I had none," she returned, "but how glad I am that we are able to be friends once again."

When the Deaths arrived some time later, I could find it in me to be sorry for his wife. Master Death was so old and wrinkled with age that he resembled nothing so much as a dried plum, his wife's vivacious beauty making the contrast between them more pointed and unkind. I had only to exchange a few words with him to discover that he was senile, whatever brains he may have had were quite withered by the years he carried and his mentality was no more than that of a child, while his rheumy, faded eyes followed the flamboyant figure of his wife with the trusting love of an infant.

Remembering Bess's words I led him to the fire and settled him in a comfortable seat away from the draughts and out of sight of his wife who was brazenly flirting with the men of the household. Even Henry Campernowne had brightened at her entrance and his laugh was ringing out loudly above the conversation as I tucked a rug across the old man's thin knees and hoped he would not notice his wife's behaviour.

We had one other guest that Christmas tide; a tall, thin man by the name of Francis Hill. He had arrived a few days earlier, ostensibly to look over some accounts belonging to the estate. His sober, black costume suited his proclaimed calling of lawyer and also that to which he truly belonged. I had no difficulty in recognising him as a Catholic priest and knew that he had come to celebrate Christmas for those of the old religion among the household.

My new gown of tawny coloured velvet had turned out well and with the pearl pendant the Queen had sent as a wedding gift hanging from the chain that already held her pearls, I felt equal to playing hostess to anyone — even Mistress Bess.

The Yule log had been dragged in and lit from the remains of last year's fire, the long refectory table in the Great Hall, used only upon such occasions, was laid with knives and silver plate, pies and platters of meat and side dishes filling the centre. Good wax candles lit the scene and I paused on the stairs, taking in the splendour of the hall below, pleased and somewhat awed to be the propagator of such magnificence.

For twelve days we roistered, eating and playing games until our appetites grew jaded and our heads and bodies ached. Each evening the hired musicians played and we danced until the candles guttered and grew dim, and I knew the heady excitement of *la Volta*, a dance much favoured by our Queen in which the men lifted their partners high into the air, causing my aunt to shut her eyes at such display and tut disapprovingly.

I was not altogether sorry when the holiday drew to an end; I found my uncle a difficult house guest, though to give him due, Conn took his entertainment upon his own shoulders. The thorn in my flesh was Bess Death. Her presence seemed to fill the house, her low, deep laugh was to be heard upon all occasions as though it floated behind her, lingering in rooms she had quitted, the heavy, cloying perfume she used hanging in the air long after she had left. Added to this was the certainty that she was cuckolding her husband. Precisely why I should come to this conclusion I do not know, save that the complacent expression she wore accorded ill with her avowed matrimonial dissatisfaction.

Only one disquieting episode occurred to upset the passing of the Holy Season and that happened late one afternoon towards the end of the holiday. I was embroidering and had taken my sewing to the wide windowseat to catch the last of the short daylight, when I heard the door behind me open and someone enter. Thinking to make my presence known I lifted a hand to the curtain that hid me, but a voice stayed the action and as I paused it became too late to show myself.

"I must leave to guide Master Gifford on his way," said a voice which I identified as belonging to Francis Hill. "I have received word that Thomas Morgan is sending him to Queen Mary with a letter of introduction in the hopes that he may be of some use to her."

"Surely he has little chance of reaching the Queen?" said my husband. "She is well guarded and has not so lenient a goaler as before."

"The queen's agent in Paris thinks highly of him. If we could establish some means of communicating with Mary it would be of immense value to our cause. As you know we have had no direct word from her for some months."

"I'll see you on your way — where do you meet him?"

Footsteps crossed the floor, the door closed and I was alone. During those few minutes the day had grown dark and my work lay unheeded in my lap. Suddenly aware of the cold, I went to the fire, holding my chilled fingers to the warmth. During the last few months I had forgotten, or chosen to ignore, my husband's involvement with the Catholic plotters, but suddenly his interests had been brought home to me and I was afraid for him.

A cold January arrived and with the twelfth day of Christmas our guests left us and travelled home. When Conn and I were alone I broached the subject that lay heavily on my mind, trying to be careful and circumspect, but by the quizzical set to his dark eyebrows, failing miserably.

"Conn," I said lightly, after one quick upward glance my gaze returning to the embroidery in my lap, "Conn, I know that that man Francis Hill was no more a lawyer than I am."

"What an astute little wife!" he commented, and fell to cracking nuts from a bowl on the table.

Recognizing the signs, I knew that the interview had started badly, but having gathered the courage to begin, could see little use in stopping. "I know as well as you he is a Catholic priest," I said boldly, and waited for his reply, smoothing the material I was sewing over my knees.

"Well?" was his uncompromising return.

I bit my lip and looked up. "I know you do not care greatly for any religion," I blurted out. "Why then, must you endanger yourself over something that means nothing to you?"

"Perditta," he said softly, "you know very little about me and I'll thank you not to meddle in my affairs, of which you know even less."

"They are my affairs, too," I cried, almost desperately and something in my voice must have reached him, for he looked at me for a while and then spoke in kinder tones.

"For all we have a queen on the throne, we live in a man's world," he said. "I do what I must and if that leads us all into danger, then I must take no account of it."

I was horrified. "You would put us all in danger, me . . . your child. Have you no thought for us? If you were taken for your beliefs, where would we be? This house, my inheritance — all would be taken to pay the fines imposed upon us."

He looked at me thoughtfully. "I'll

not be taken by the priest takers," he said. "I'll give you my word upon that, wife."

"Soldiers, then. The Queen's men even."

He raised his eyebrows. "Why should the military be interested in me?"

I lowered my gaze so as not to meet his keen eyes. "Most Catholics want Mary Stuart on the throne of England. I fear that if you are involved with one faction, you *must* by that very action, be involved with the other."

The room was very quiet. I refused to look up, knowing that my husband's gaze was on my bowed head. At last he spoke, his quiet voice making me start.

"What sharp little ears you have," he remarked unpleasantly. "There's an old saying, listening at keyholes does the listener no good."

"I didn't — " I said, involuntarily.

"Hiding behind curtains comes to the same thing."

"Oh, Conn, I'm sorry," I told him. "I did not mean to, it was purely by accident . . . and I've been so worried."

"Good — perhaps it will teach you not to listen to other people's conversations," my husband said unkindly.

"I'd much prefer that you were not involved with my uncle's machinations. I am afraid of him and of what he might do. He has no honour or kindness. If he were taken he would tell all in an attempt to save his own skin."

"How sensible then, to tell him only that which he needs to know."

I was relieved for a minute, before another worry struck me. "Henry Campernowne is of very little account beside the Queen of Scots," I said soberly.

"True, but Mary, poor soul, is tucked away in Tutbury Castle under the unloving care of Sir Amias Paulet, a gentleman who has tight care of his royal prisoner."

I looked up. "You think these plots and counterplots will have little success?"

"I think they may encompass her death," was his bleak reply and upon his words I fell silent, having much to think about.

Spring came and with it, a fine pearl

from my royal Godparent. I heard that Mary Stuart had been moved to Chartley, some fifteen miles north of Tutbury, but the matter roused little interest in me. I was growing round and plump and could find little of importance save the babe I was carrying. Cousin Jane was allowed to visit me and in her company I found much enjoyment. Conn and I settled into something like contented marriage, only now and again sharpening our claws upon each other. I took easily to wedded life and if I wished sometimes for the wild distractions of the love about which the poets talked, usually I was contented with my lot and if the traffic of priests or Catholic messengers through my house continued, I did my best to ignore their true business and treat them as passing travellers.

Luckily, I had had the forethought to bring my mother's recipe book with me from Somerset and that summer I paid heed to my role of housewife and dried and preserved the fruits of the countryside and our gardens to the best of my ability, finding somewhat to my surprise that the task was much to my liking. Bess Death paid a few neighbourly calls, but after her Christmas visit, seemed to have little wish to further our friendship. However, the last time she rode over she told me that she was pregnant, appearing pleased at the prospect of motherhood, while I fleetingly pondered upon the identity of the father.

My own babe was due in August and having arranged for the local midwife, an aged crone but tolerably clean, and begged leave for Jane to be with me, I settled back to await the great event. So certain was I that my child would be well and strong that I flouted convention and refused to put black mourning bands ready with the swaddling clothes. Jane said I was right not to contemplate the grimmer aspects of pregnancy, but both she and I knew, although we did not speak of such things, that the time ahead was dangerous. Many women died in childbed or later fell victim to the puerperal fever, while if the first child lived it was considered extremely lucky.

Luck must have been with me, for one

day towards the middle of July, I caught my heel in my gown and was brought to my knees in the garden. Jane was with me and trying to keep our wits about us, she helped me back to the house. At first all seemed well, but later that day my pains took me and the next morning I was safely delivered. Despite her precipitous entry into this world my daughter took tight hold on life and ignoring all precedents, throve.

Conn seemed not to care about her sex, declaring himself glad we were both well.

"I had wished for a blackheaded son," I whispered from the bed, as my husband took the babe to the window the better to admire her.

He sent me a smile across the room. "Instead of which you have a redheaded daughter."

"Do you mind?" I asked anxiously, knowing how much store men put upon having an heir.

"Not at all," he said, handing the babe to the nurse. "I own I'd like a boy but we have plenty of time to fill our nursery."

I was satisfied with his words, turning my head to study the crumpled features of my baby. "Elizabeth suits her," I said, sleep threatening to overcome me. "It's a good time to flatter the Queen."

6

DESPITE the premature birth, my strength returned quickly and soon I was able to leave my bed and sit beside the open window enjoying the sunshine and the view of my garden, while I suckled the babe or sewed tiny garments.

It was from this window that I looked up one afternoon to see the black figure of Francis Hill, riding up like a portent of doom. Drawing back with fast beating heart, I hid in the shadows of my room and watched his arrival, wondering what business brought him to Galliard's Hay.

Whatever it was it could not have taken long to dispense for he rode away well before evening, leaving Conn free to visit me as usual. Making no attempt to hide my knowledge, as soon as we were alone I asked the reason for the priest's call.

"Don't grow too curious, sweetheart," he advised lightly.

"As your wife I have a right to know," I said stubbornly.

"In the law wives have very few rights — I could beat you if I liked. Your inheritance now belongs to me. If I wished I could remove the child from your care and lock you away from the world."

He spoke thoughtfully, his voice mild and light, but knowing the truth of his words, they filled me with dismay. I watched him fearfully as he looked down at the baby, seeming to concentrate all his attention on the small sleeping bundle.

"You wouldn't?" I asked at last, one hand pressed to my fast beating heart.

He looked up as I spoke, his gaze cold and withdrawn as he eyed me and even after all these months I was shaken to meet with the stranger I had married.

"Control your curiosity, wife." His voice was curt and I shivered a little under his icy gaze. "There may be happenings in this house that puzzle you, arrivals and departures that fill you with curiosity. Knowing your character, I realize full well that you will be filled

130

with the desire to pry into others' affairs. Take my advice, Perditta, and remember that your wish to delve into secrets has already led you into danger. I may not be able to, or may not have the wish to, protect you again."

I was silent, clasping my hands in my lap and staring down at my trembling fingers. Conn left the cradle and went to stand by the window.

"I leave for London tomorrow," he announced abruptly and I looked up quickly, connecting the two happenings.

Reading my expression, he shook his head slowly, a slight smile playing about his mouth. "No, sweetheart, nothing to do with Master Hills' visit. I merely wish for a likeness to be taken of my wife and having heard much of Nicholas Hilliard, the Queen's painter, I am resolved to seek him out and ask him to undertake the task."

"A portrait? Of me?" I was unable to hide my astonishment.

Conn was amused by my reaction to his announcement. "Why so surprised?" he asked. "You'd look well in a jewel to hang about my neck. From all I hear of

Master Hilliard's work, not only will it be decorative but it will be an inheritance to leave our children." For a moment longer he looked down at me, his expression unfathomable, before abruptly turning away, pausing at the door to speak over his shoulder. "Take care while I'm away, Perditta . . . remember what I said."

He was away almost a full month and much was to happen during that time, proving that even our sleepy corner of Hampshire can be caught up in events of import. At first all was calm and the even rhythm of our days only enlivened by the event of my leaving my chamber and coming down stairs to take the running of the household back into my own hands, but some time in early August, Dudley rode over from Hawks' Hill, his face proclaiming the serious nature of his business.

"Conn is in London," I told him in answer to his query and asked boldly why he wanted to see him.

He had been thrown into agitation by Sir Conn's absence and now my innocent question appeared to disturb him even further. One look at his pale countenance and visibly shaking hands convincing me of the importance of his mission.

"Come into the parlour," I said abruptly and taking wine and goblets from the hall cupboard, ushered him into the inner room and closed the door behind us. Pressing him into a chair I poured wine and placed it in front of him. "You'd best tell me what brings you here," I told him. "Is my uncle ill?"

Gulping down the wine, he shook his head. Suddenly burying his head in his hands, his shoulders heaved and I thought he was crying, before I realized that he was shaking with fear. I put my hand on his shoulder in silent sympathy and he started up like a nervous horse, his eyes wide and wild with fright.

"What is it? *Tell* me!" I cried, nearly as fearful as he was.

"How can I? You're not one of us!"

"Us?" I frowned, before catching his meaning. "Catholic you mean?"

He nodded and understanding something of the matter that had brought him to Galliard's Hay, I sank down into a chair and stared blankly before me. "Dear God!" I breathed and closed my eyes in

133

silent prayer, before turning my attention back to my cousin at the end of the table. "I . . . have some idea of what goes on in our houses," I said, as calmly as I was able. "If this matter involves Conn then I think you had best tell me. Remember I am his wife and kin to you and would do none of you any harm."

He studied my face for one agonized moment longer, before bursting out, "It's the Scottish Queen! There is a plot — and an incriminating letter. One that will do her much harm. We have just heard that all has been discovered, that the conspirators are taken by Walsingham's men! My father sent me to warn Sir Conn — "

I drew a shaking breath. "Is . . . he involved?" I asked painfully and scarcely needed Dudley's nod to know the answer. Biting my lip, I forced my brain to function, seeking for some way out of this blow that had fallen on our family. "I'll send a trusted servant with a message to Conn — and remove all signs of recusancy here. I know where the priest keeps his vestments and books. Unless your parents wish otherwise I think it best that Jane stays here, I can pass her off as a visitor."

Dudley nodded agreement and seemed willing to let me make any arrangement. I eyed him thoughtfully, wondering how he would react to my next suggestion. "If I give you a purse of money, you could ride to the coast and be out of the country by morning," I offered, tentatively.

He looked up, but to my surprise shook his head, climbing to his feet with all the weariness of an old man. "My thanks, cousin," he said, "but my place is at home with my parents. I only came to warn Sir Conn. I know I can trust you to take what care you can of Jane."

Meeting my eyes, he gave me a tired smile and realizing the effort it cost him, I felt more kindly towards him than I had ever done before.

As soon as he had left, I scribbled a hasty note to Conn and directing it to Sir Robert's lodgings, put it into the hands of a trusty servant, urging him to use all speed on his way to London. I then went in search of Jane to prepare her for possible happenings.

The next few days put an almost intolerable strain on us, every sound making our pulses race, while we strained our ears and listened for any unusual noise. At last came the sound we had been dreading and both Jane and I started to our feet, staring wide-eyed at each other as horses dashed into the courtyard.

Scarcely daring to breath, we waited for the thunderous knocking which would proclaim the arrival of soldiers, but instead heard feet cross the Great Hall and the parlour door was flung open to reveal the tall figure of Sir Conn.

Heedless of the mud and dust that mired his clothes speaking of his headlong ride, I flung myself into his arms, relieved beyond measure that he was safe home again.

"Why, wife, what is it? he asked softly, holding me in a comforting embrace.

"Oh, Conn — I thought you were lodged in the Tower!"

"Not I," he said with the conviction of his own infallability.

"Did you get my message? Walsingham's

men might come even now . . . Should you be here?"

He laughed and put me into a chair. "Calm yourself, Perditta. I do assure you that you have no cause for alarm. For the love her father bore mine, the Queen will treat me kindly."

"Even though . . . Dudley said there was a plot, to put the Scottish Queen on the throne. I suppose Elizabeth could never forgive such a thing."

"No." he agreed thoughtfully. "I fear that Mary Stuart may have done herself more harm than she realizes."

"What of my father?" put in Jane, who until now had listened in silence. "I fear he is involved."

Sir Conn looked up quickly. "Are you sure? I thought he was wiser than to dabble in such affairs." He looked questioningly at her, but she sighed, raising her shoulders in a helpless gesture. "I'll ride over tomorrow to see what I can find out," he told her. "Don't worry, Walsingham will be after bigger fish than your father."

But in the event, he proved wrong. Just as he was drawing on his gauntlets prior to setting out for Hawks' Hill, a commotion in the courtyard made us glance at each other. In a stride, he was at the door and had flung it wide, while Jane and I hovered behind, peering round his shoulders, half afraid to look.

A heavy foursquare coach, its horses steaming and foam flecked from the speed with which they had been driven, was pulled up askew beside the steps, while the distraught figure of my aunt had pushed the half-door open, flinging herself out of the coach and tumbled to her knees on the cobbles.

Hurrying down the steps, we raised her to her feet and supported her into the house, while she panted and sobbed and uttered disjointed sentences.

At last she was calm enough to tell us what had happened and looking at her hair all undone and her clothes dishevelled and untidy, I was moved to sympathy and held her hand in a comforting grip while she told her story.

The soldiers had come early in the morning before anyone was astir, bursting in and running through the house before the household was awake enough to deny them entry. The priestly vestments were soon found, but this was a minor affair, Henry Campernowne had been implicated in the plot for the throne and once the house was searched, had been arrested and carried off to London, Dudley voluntarily accompanying his father in order to bring back news. For the first time I heard mention of the Babbington plot, Babbington being the name of the young man who had instituted and arranged the whole matter.

Suddenly my aunt turned to me, grasping my hand and holding my eyes with the intensity of her emotion. "You must do something, niece," she said, fiercely. "If the estate is confiscated we shall be destitute. You must tell the queen that I am her loyal subject, that my husband forced me to acquiesce in this business — that I had no say in the matter. Write a letter and Dudley shall present it to her, I hear she has an eye for a pretty young man."

I drew back, releasing my hand with difficulty from her bruising grip, as I realized that her anxiety was not for her husband as I had supposed, but for herself and her son.

"I shall write and plead for leniency for my uncle," I told her quietly. "More I cannot do."

She leaned forward, her eyes staring into mine. "You must tell her that the family is loyal — that he constrained us to act against our wishes."

I looked to Conn for guidance, but he was standing at the window, his back to the room, and seemed aloof from the proceedings behind him.

I shook my head. "No — I will write and sue for her kindness, but I cannot give my word for that which is not true."

The look Mistress Campernowne gave me was filled with malice and fury, but before she could speak Conn came to stand behind my chair, one hand on my shoulder.

"Let me advise you, mistress, to return to your home," he said evenly. "With the soldiery still on the premises it would be unwise to leave it open and under the care only of servants."

For a few seconds she stared at us

both, her look so malevolent that I was glad of my husband's steady presence.

"I'll take Jane with me — I have need of a daughter's presence," she said at last, taking the only means at her disposal to hurt me.

When they had gone, my aunt stoney-faced with worry and rage at being denied her desire and poor Jane pale, but striving for calm to face her mother's cruelty, I turned to Conn.

"Was I right?" I asked. "*Should* I have lied for her?"

"I had not expected a wife with such a deep sense of honour. I imagined it was something few women possessed."

"I would lie for someone I loved," I told him, truthfully. "It would be a different matter then, I think . . . so you see, I am not at all an honourable person."

He smiled. "Leave honour and other such foolish things to men. I often believe them highly overrated myself."

"Will you go to London?"

"Not I. I have a notion that we might have a visit from Walsingham's men. It would be unlike the Secretary of State to miss the opportunity of searching as many houses as he can contrive while his men are in the neighborhood. I must go and make certain that there is nothing for them to find."

"If you mean the vestments in the attic, I have already removed them."

He turned at my words, his eyes suddenly narrow and watchful. "How resourceful of you, wife. Pray tell me where you have put them."

"I had Little John, when he was here, construct me a little hideyhole in my bedchamber."

Conn viewed me, his expression taut with an emotion I could not read. "And where is this hide of yours?"

I answered him readily. "In the wainscotting behind the bed. Master John did a very good job."

Sir Conn considered, studying me thoughtfully. "Certainly I've never seen it. I wonder why you have never felt the need to mention it; however, I suppose I must be glad you kept your wits."

"Would you rather I had lost them?" I asked, lifting my chin at his tone.

"I'd like to know how you had

knowledge of their whereabouts."

"If you think someone told me about the vestments, you forget, husband, that I have had experience before of where your priests hide their belongings. I only had to look for a loose floorboard in the attic. It seems to me that a more original turn of mind would be of use in your secret matters."

"I'll have a word with the next Jesuit I see — "

Our raised voices hung in the atmosphere and suddenly aware that we were shouting, we fell silent and stared at each other.

"Write your letter, Perditta," Conn said abruptly, marching to the door, "and I'll arrange for a man to take it to London."

Sir Conn's fears were justified, for the next day a troop of horsemen rode up to Galliard's Hay and demanded entrance. My husband met them at the door, heard out their leader and quietly bade them enter and search to their heart's content. Apparently fearing nothing, he bore the gentleman in charge into the parlour and offering him refreshments, closed the door. I was not made of such stern stuff and hovered anxiously while the soldiers pried into every room and every nook and cranny they could find. My heart quickened when they knocked and felt the panelling in the Great Hall, but apart from peering cursorily inside the cupboard it held no interest for them. I waited uneasily while they searched the house and outbuildings, but what with the weather being seasonably hot and my having had the forethought to order a cask of ale broached for their benefit, their hearts were not in the matter and they soon gathered in the courtyard, wiping their lips and eager to rest while they awaited orders.

"You, my wife, are a crafty wench," Conn told me as we watched them ride off, something approaching admiration in his voice.

"Poor men. Anyone could see they were weary and thirsty enough to drink a barrel dry."

He laughed and clapped me close against his side, tucking me under his arm and we went back into the house, closer physically and mentally than we had been for some time, but our unity was not to continue. A few days later our content was disturbed and by so trifling a matter that I was puzzled anew by the enigma that I had married.

The Deaths had sent us a silver porringer as a Christening gift for Elizabeth and not to be outdone in neighbourliness, as they too had been blessed with a child, I selected a spoon from my bridegifts and proposed to take it to them with our thanks. To my surprise Conn firmly vetoed the whole idea.

"But why ever not?" I asked, bewildered by his attitude. "The soldiers are long gone and there can be no danger so near to home and with our men to escort me."

"I don't wish it," was all he would say until at last I lost my temper, stamped my foot and cried that I *would* go.

At that he turned upon me. "Obey me, woman," he said wrathfully and for a moment, I thought he would strike me. Bewildered by the turn of events and the suddenness of our quarrel, I could only stare at him. In a voice of a man goaded beyond endurance he said that he would take it later and with a face like thunder flung himself from the room.

Watching as he rode off as though all the hounds of hell were at his heels, I lost no time in ordering a horse saddled and still hot with rage, set off myself in the direction of Priory Hall, the Death's house. After a few miles I was cool enough to begin to feel qualms about my action, but comforted myself that Conn had been unreasonable and deserved a little wifely disobedience to show that I was no mere chattle to do his bidding. My heart fluttering a little at the thought of his rage to come, I rode on and was soon at Master Death's property.

I had been there before and so scarcely spared the ornate building a glance; red brick and barley twist chimneys held little interest for me at that moment, beset as I was with doubts about the wiseness of my visit. Bess Death and I were hardly friends and suddenly the idea of exchanging gifts for our babes seemed hypocritical beyond measure.

However, I could hardly ride away again and leaving my horse with the groom who had ridden with me, I made my business known and soon the mistress of the house appeared to attend me.

"Why, Lady Galliard," she cooed. "What a delight to see you." She glanced behind me and raised her eyebrows.

"Sir Conn presents his apologies," I said bluntly. "I'm afraid he had business matters."

She gave a brittle laugh and assured me she had not looked to see my husband. "Why it's only a few days since he was here."

I looked up at that, hiding my chagrin that Conn had not thought to make his visit known to me. "I came to thank you for the Christening gift," I said somewhat stiffly, "and bring you one for your own baby."

"How glad I am that our babies arrived safely. I daresay Conn was a little disappointed in being presented with a girl. Men I know look for a son to ensure the continuance of their name."

"Conn is very pleased with Elizabeth," I told her. "In fact he quite dotes on her."

She gave a little trill of laughter. "*That* I cannot imagine." She paused and looked at me speculatively. "You know I had a boy?" she asked, not bothering to hide the triumphant note in her voice.

"You said so in your letter," I reminded her.

"Of course." She turned to lead the way upstairs, talking volubly over her shoulder all the while. "Come and see the baby. My husband has showered me with gifts — I vow he quite thought fatherhood was beyond him and he's delighted to have been proved wrong."

She opened a door and a woman rose from beside the cradle at our entrance and retired to a discreet distance.

"Come and admire my son, Lady Galliard," said Mistress Death, her voice high and excited and a little breathless, making me wonder at her obvious emotion. "Tell me if you do not think him a wonder. So dark and strong, I vow he looks a man already."

Her eyes held mine, wide and sparkling. Puzzled by her mood and worried by some instinct, I dropped my eyes reluctantly to the cradle as she drew back the coverings, exposing the child to my gaze.

Catching my breath I stared at the baby and could have been gazing at a miniture copy of my husband; the same thick, black hair, identical nose and mouth, even the shape of his head and chin were the same. Suddenly the baby opened his eyes and, dizzy with relief, I found myself looking into a dark blue gaze.

"Their eyes change, you know," said the woman beside me significantly. "They all have eyes that colour. I daresay he will have quite pale eyes later."

Struggling for control, I fought to hide my feelings and gripped the nearby tabletop until my knuckles gleamed white. "He's — very handsome," I said at last, and even to myself my voice sounded weak and shook noticeably.

"My dear Lady Galliard, are you ill?" asked Bess Death, assuming concern. "Pray, sit down and let me procure you a glass of wine."

"I am quite well," I assured her, but she and the nurse insisted on fussing over me and all the while I was aware of her hardly concealed triumph.

I drank wine and ate cakes, making conversation and exchanging pleasantries, only my pride keeping me from screaming and striking at that beautiful, smiling face.

At last I made my excuses and escaped, hoping that I had concealed the wild turmoil of emotions I felt from the enquiring gaze of the chatelaine of Priory Hall. Unwilling to give her any satisfaction by admitting my own pain, I hid my hurt until I was well away from her triumphant eyes, setting heels into my mount's sides and riding back to Galliard's Hay with little attention for safety or comfort.

Arriving in the courtyard, breathless and dishevelled, I flung my reins to a groom and ran at once to my chamber, heedless of the servants' interest. Dusk was falling when I heard Conn ride over the cobbles below my window and I rose quickly from the bed where I had been sitting and shot the bolt across the door.

A few minutes later the latch lifted. "Perditta?" called Conn's voice. "Open this door." He waited a few seconds before rattling the latch impatiently. "Open the door," he repeated, "or I will break it down."

Knowing he would keep his word, I hesitated only a moment, before abruptly sliding the bolt back and crossing the room to stare out at the darkening garden as he entered. He closed the door behind him and stood with his back to it, the silence heavy and oppressive.

"So you went," he said at last, not deigning to act out a subterfuge.

"I saw Mistress Death's baby," I said, my voice falsely high and bright. "Such a handsome, *dark* child — one could never be in doubt of his fatherhood. I'm afraid it's written all over his visage!"

"Say it to me as you must, but never let me hear it abroad."

"Are you so nice about your mistress' honour?" I flung at him, turning from the window.

"Not hers — *yours*."

"I would say it was a little late for such a care," I cried, noting with a heavy dismay that he had not bothered to deny the accusation; until then I had nursed a slight hope that the evidence of my eyes would prove a coincidence. I had even known the hope that there might be a common ancestor to make reasonable the child's likeness to my husband. "The child is yours. Don't deny it for it's there for all the world to see and recognize."

He pushed his shoulders away from the door. "It's over and done with — " he began.

"So much over that you called upon her a few days ago," I accused, my voice shrill.

"To tell her that all was over between us — "

"You even invited her here for Christmas. I knew her poor old husband was being cuckolded, but I never thought it was by you. Oh, Conn . . . in my own house!"

He shook his head, not meeting my eyes. "I wasn't the only man in the house," he said, heavily. "I finished with Mistress Death before that."

"And yet her babe is the same age as mine and you feel the need to visit her, still."

"Your child was early, have you

152

forgot?" Suddenly his anger matched mine. "I called on her, because she asked me to and — thinking she had some trouble I felt an obligation to her."

"You thought her husband had realized, you mean."

Before I was aware of his intentions, he had crossed the floor, with the silent quickness big men so often have and seized me by the arms above the elbows. "Mind your tongue, wife," he snarled, shaking me ruthlessly. "I have given you an explanation — I make no excuses to anyone, least of all to you. I am my own master. If you think to wear the breeches, then sweetheart, you've married the wrong man."

Releasing me so abruptly that I reeled and fell against the wall, he smiled down at me, his eyes pale, narrowed slits. "I should be flattered, I suppose, that you are so jealous."

"Jealous!" I cried, staring up at him with wide-eyed rage. "Of you, Conn Galliard? I care naught for Bess Death's leavings!"

The smile left his face leaving it suddenly pale and taut, while his eyes grew ice-cold and hard. "Don't try me too far, Perditta," he warned quietly, in a tone that sent a shiver down my spine.

"I'll go farther," I said, ignoring the promptings of fear that were nudging me. "From now I'll no longer share my bed with you." Knowing I was going too far, goading the man before me into an act we would both regret, but wishing to hurt him as he had hurt me, I hurled defiance at him. "Go back to your drab — I'll have none of you."

For a moment I thought he would kill me. He towered over me, his hands raised and a look of murder on his face, before his mouth curved in a devilish smile and he pulled me roughly against him, locking my wrists behind me for all I fought with all my strength.

"Don't think to give the orders, sweetheart," he said softly, pulling off my coif and tossing it aside as he twisted his fingers in my hair. "Remember you are my wife and so submissive in law to my wishes and desires."

Abruptly I stopped struggling and fell against him. "Conn, don't — please don't," I begged, knowing whilst I pleaded that it was useless.

Even as I spoke his fingers tightened in my hair, dragging my head back as he kissed me, roughly and cruelly. Then lifting me as easily as if I had been a child he swung me up into his arms and bore me to the bed.

For a moment he looked down into my frightened face, his eyes glittering in the dusk, his teeth gleaming against his dark skin.

"I think we have both learned a lesson today," he said, "on the same subject; you, my love, that an obedient wife is the happiest and I that the reins I've allowed you have been far too long. From now on, Perditta, I intend to be master in Galliard's Hay and you will learn to be my dutiful, loving wife."

He tossed me into the bed and before I could slither away across the silk cover he reached out and pulled me back into his arms.

7

FOR the first time I realized the monstrous inequality of a woman's position. However much I railed against man-made laws there was nothing I could do; if I ran away no-one would give me sanctuary against my husband, my inheritance belonged to the man I had married, he could lock me up, beat me — even take away my child and in the eyes of the law he was doing no wrong.

Aware of my thoughts, Conn laughed at my frustrations, ignoring the growing dislike that I felt for him and went on his way, whistling as though he knew not a care in the world.

Which was totally untrue, for I knew he had received a news sheet that had disturbed him mightily. It had contained news of the recent plot, stating in horrifying detail how Anthony Babbington and his fellow conspiritors had met their death at the executioner's bloody hands.

I had gone to him then and speaking willingly to him for the first time in many weeks, had asked fearfully if that would be my uncle's fate.

He shook his head and sighed, crumpling the ill-printed paper in his hand. "You should not have read it," he told me heavily. "It does not concern you."

"I have a right to know," I said indignantly. "I am not a fool. A woman, yes, but why you should think that makes me a dotard I do not know."

"How your father must have regretted that you were not a boy," Conn said, his tone softening slightly and his gaze more kind than it had been of late.

"Do you know if my uncle is likely to — to — ," I asked stiffly, ignoring his overture.

"To suffer in a like manner," he finished for me, his voice harsh, the momentary tenderness forgotten. "I do not know. Not having received an answer from the queen, I know no more than you."

Now that his rejected sympathy was withdrawn I wished for it and hovered uncertainly beside his chair.

"But — what do you think?" I insisted.

His eyes were bleak. "I think the queen will have his life, but perhaps not in so barbarous a manner as those directly involved in the plot . . . after all, Henry Campernowne can hardly have been in the forefront. He has neither the brains nor the wealth needed for such a venture." He beat a tattoo on the table with his fingernails, deep in thought. "I'll journey to London to find out what news I can. Doubtless Dudley could do with a friend."

"It might be wiser not to proclaim our kinship," I warned him reluctantly.

He shrugged indifferently. "Perhaps . . . nevertheless, I've a mind to visit the capital."

I opened my mouth to speak, to say that I would rather he stayed at home, that some instinct warned me that trouble lay ahead, but he pushed back his chair and strode from the room before I could utter any of my forebodings, and the warnings died on my lips.

Almost at once my instincts were proved right; before noon on the day that he left, a trusted servant whispered in my ear that someone wished to see me in the stables. Warned by his manner, I asked no questions, but made my way casually out of the house to find an exhausted horse and his anxious rider hidden in the gloomy depths of the stables.

"Who are you — what do you want?" I asked sharply, recognizing the unwelcome form of the priest Francis Hill, as he came forward out of the shadows.

"I need shelter," he said, his voice hurried and nervous. "The soldiers are close behind — "

"And you came here?"

"Believe me, only the utmost need makes me put friends in danger. I carry a vital message, which must get to its destination."

I took in his nervous manner, starting at every sound, always watching the door and yet recognizing the iron determination within the man, and viewed him with respect. Making up my mind, I issued orders for the horse to be hidden in the nearby wood, remembering thankfully the deep road overhung by trees that would have hidden his approach, and taking his arm urged him into the house.

As I latched the secret back on the hidden room and closed the cupboard door, hooves clattered into the courtyard behind me and I turned as the front door was thrust open and men spilled into the house.

"Sir Robert!" I gasped in surprised relief as the queen's man thrust his way through the soldiers.

The bow he made me was sketchy and his face inscrutible, with none of the friendliness I expected to see.

"We are here on Her Majesty's business," he said coldly, pulling the gauntlets from his hands and beating them against one palm. "A charge has been laid against you."

"W-what charge?" I asked and to my dismay heard my voice shake.

"Hiding a Jesuit," he answered briefly. "One involved with the Scottish Queen."

Now I understood the message Francis Hill carried and grew chill with fear even as some corner of my brain asked how anyone could have known he would come to Galliard's Hay.

"You'll find no-one here," I assured

Sir Robert more stoutly than I felt.

Turning away from me he gave orders to his men and they left in noisy groups to search the house and grounds. Sir Robert Varley walked about the Great Hall, examining the panelling, but avoiding my eyes and obviously ill at ease.

"Will you take some wine?" I offered, moving casually towards the cupboard.

He shook his head, and remembering the other search when the leader had been only too willing to sample Conn's liquor, I knew with a sinking heart that this visit must be more serious.

"Are we not still friends?" I asked in a low voice.

Sir Robert sighed. "I gave my pledge to the Queen," he said quietly. "My word to her comes above all things — even friendship. If you were my kin and I found evidence here, I would arrest you. Believe me I would regret it deeply, but would have no compunction about carrying it out."

I gave him a strained smile. "How lucky then, that you will find nothing," I said, striving for lightness.

"Believe me, Lady Galliard, nothing

will please me more."

I dropped him a curtsey and left the room, thinking that to remain longer might arouse suspicions. Sitting in the inner parlour, I calmed my nervous fears as best I could whilst listening to the sounds of the search. This was much more thorough than the somewhat cursory hunt we had sustained before. Sir Robert obviously disliked the necessity and because of his dislike, would hunt and probe more thoroughly. Knowing his intelligence, I resisted the temptation to offer the soldiers wine as I had before and tried to go about my normal daily duties, ignoring the upsetting presence of the rough soldiery as best I could.

At last, as evening was falling, it was over and Robert Varley came to me, acknowledging that he had found nothing incriminating.

"Pray accept my apologies," he said, bowing.

"Are we friends again?" I asked.

"If you'll have me," he answered ruefully.

For a moment we looked at each other and then I impulsively put out my hand.

"I'd prefer to have you as a friend than an enemy," I told him, truthfulness in my voice. "The evening comes on a pace — will you stay the night?" I asked, knowing that I would have made the offer under normal circumstances and that not to do so might awaken suspicions in his astute mind.

He smiled down at me. "I hoped you would invite me," he said, "then I would know that I was truly forgiven."

"Your men can use the stables," I told him, hoping that the groom would have the sense not to return the priest's horse until all was clear. "We'll have dinner in the inner parlour, while your room is set to rights — I'm afraid it is none too tidy at the moment, like all my chambers, it looks as if a wild wind had blown through it."

At my orders the servants began to lay the table in the inner room, the smells of roast meat and pies carrying pleasantly to our nostrils as we talked and I spared a thought for the hungry priest incarcerated behind the panelling.

"Why did you come?" I asked, when the servants had gone, bearing the

163

remains of the meat dishes and leaving us alone to our sweet course.

Sir Robert looked uncomfortable. "Information was laid against you — that you had a Jesuit in hiding here."

I raised my eyebrows, making mental note that the information Sir Robert had given me would make it easy to discover the person who ill-wished us and remarked lightly, "How singularly ill-informed."

"Nevertheless, it had to be investigated. Mary's abortive plot has brought much unpleasantness in its train and with your uncle involved . . . I am afraid you were easily suspect. Do you know you have an enemy in the district? I cannot name her to you, but I can warn you to be careful."

I pricked my ears at his use of the feminine gender. "I have a notion who it may be," I remarked quietly, thinking of my aunt and remembering her vindictive expression the last time we had met.

"Conn, you say, is in London?" He went on at my brief nod. "I hope all goes well with him."

"Does anything ever go awry for him?"

I questioned, unable to keep the bitterness out of my voice and the man opposite looked up, his eyes keen.

"If I were a heathen, I would think him born under a lucky star," I went on.

"Is all not well between you? I had thought you happy when I was here at Christmas."

I lifted my shoulders and let them fall. "So had I, but lately I've learned what an innocent, unwordly simpleton I was."

Sir Robert looked at me and away, making to speak but changing his mind, until at last he rose and coming to where I sat, took my hand in his, breaking into quick, impassioned speech.

"Perditta — when I thought you happy I could not speak, I could not tell you what my feelings were, but knowing what I now do and understanding something of your unhappiness, I feel able to declare myself. Perditta, I love you, I would have asked for your hand, save that Sir Conn won you too quickly."

I looked at him sadly, not surprised by his outburst. I had liked him from the first and had suspected that our relationship would deepen given the opportunity. For

165

all his air of fashionable gallantry there was something vulnerable about him, a certain gentleness that attracted me, especially now that I had tasted my husband's ruthless indifference to my feelings or wishes.

Hesitantly, I reached out a hand and touched Sir Robert's bowed blond head and at once my hand was taken and pressed to his lips.

"I knew you were not indifferent," he whispered.

"Oh, no!" I said softly and let him take me in his arms, my whole being crying out for the comfort and security he could provide and of which I was in so much need.

His kisses were sweet and gentle, not arousing me to passion as Conn's did, but awakening in me a slow, gentle joy.

"What are we to do?" I cried at last, drawing back. "If only my uncle . . . if only Conn — "

I told him then the tale of my marriage and how I had been forced into it, forgetting in my misery the times when Conn and I had been happy, remembering only his harshness

166

and demanding ways.

"The fellow's a blackguard!" Sir Robert exclaimed. "If I take this sorry tale to the Queen — "

"Oh, no, pray do not," I cried, thankful that I had neglected to mention Conn's part in the Catholic service held in my uncle's attic.

"He's obviously implicated — the marriage could be annulled."

"I have a babe," I reminded him.

"Yes," he said, sighing. "I had . . . thought to find a way out of our difficulties."

For a moment we looked at each other, our longing clearly written on both our faces, but when he took me in his arms again, I made a slight gesture of repudiation which he did not notice.

He held me against his chest, speaking above my head. "Cannot we find . . . some happiness?"

A while before and I would have denied him nothing, but now I had returned to my senses. The mention of my husband's name had brought him to mind and remembering his forceful personality and ruthless care of all that was his, I knew that I could not deceive him and put Robert in danger, for I knew with all my heart that if I did so, Conn would surely kill him. Besides, some lingering memory of the affection I had held for him remained, making me reluctant to take the final irretrievable step away from him.

"I am not a light woman," I told Sir Robert, speaking with difficulty and avoiding his gaze. "I could not deceive my husband and remain here, neither could I leave my daughter and he would never let me take her away from Galliard's Hay."

Sir Robert's kiss was gentle and catching his hands in mine, I held them to my cheek, closing my eyes against the gathering tears.

"We must forget all that has passed," I told him. "You must promise me not to use what I have told you against him."

He held my face between his hands, making me look at him. "You have my word," he said simply.

"We must talk of other things." Wiping away the wayward tears that slipped down my cheeks, I smoothed my hair and set my gown to rights, searching the while for a topic of conversation that would ease the emotion between us.

"The Scottish Queen?" I asked at last. "What of her?"

"She has been removed to Fotheringhay Castle," he told me, accepting my lead. "No doubt she will be put on trial."

"Trial?" I repeated, my interest taken. "But she is a queen — surely such cannot be tried like any other mortal?"

"So she contends, but Elizabeth would have it differently and as she is all powerful, will doubtless have her way. Walsingham engineered all this, you know. He is a master of intrigue, with spies everywhere. He even knew an attempt was being made to get in touch with Mary and managed to convert the man and through him arrange that all Mary's mail was read by the Queen's men. In one of her letters she agreed to Elizabeth's murder!"

Forgetting my own trouble, I stared at him. "But that will mean — !"

"The death sentence," he finished for me, his face unusually grim. "Much as the thought of executing an annointed queen is distasteful to all, we must admit that it would be safer for the country to have only one queen within its bounds. Mary Stuart is a constant source of danger, a rallying point for Catholic extremists within our very realm — and now that she has pledged herself to agree to Her Majesty's death — " He spread his hands wide. "I am afraid that she has signed her own execution order."

I sat down slowly, filled with compassion for this unknown woman. "But to have been held a prisoner all these years . . . " I murmured. "To have known no freedom since she left Scotland, must have been intolerable."

"Don't waste your pity, Perditta," Sir Robert told me and gone was the gentle lover of a few minutes before, in his place a grim-faced man without sympathy. "She has been the death of many men, even her own husband so it's said.

"Let us hope that this plot does not lead to Catholic prosecutions," went on Sir Robert, echoing my thoughts. "One would have thought that the old religion and the new could live side by side without hate and fear, but it seems it is not so."

"Surely all people should be united?" I asked fiercely.

"Humans, my dear, are full of failings. Greed, envy, bigotry . . . I fear we are all a prey to such emotions."

He looked down at me, a smile on his lips, but such sadness in his eyes that I caught my breath and involuntarily reached out a hand towards him. Taking it, he placed a kiss within the palm and folded my fingers over it.

"If it had been otherwise I would have wished for no other happiness than to call you wife," he said, his voice soft. "As it is, I must ask your forgiveness for having made my feelings known and for having caused you pain. This must be a matter between us alone, but if you should ever need me in any way, pray believe me a friend with your welfare at heart and ever ready to put myself at your command."

A moment longer he gazed at me, before bowing, and then he turned and quickly left the room. I watched him go with very mixed emotions; I wanted him to turn back and carry me away like a knight of old and yet knew that if he was to propose such an act, I would repulse him. One treacherous part of my mind reminded me that Conn would have had no time for scruples and would have borne me off willynilly if he had desired me.

As soon as Sir Robert and his men had left the next morning I let the priest out of his hiding-place and saw him on his way with a sigh of thankfulness at his departure. By the time my husband returned both he and Sir Robert were long gone, but it did not take Conn long to learn of the baronet's presence.

"Why did you not tell me you had a visitor?" he demanded.

"I would have done so," I answered coolly, "but it seems there is no need, since someone else took the duty upon himself."

He looked somewhat disconcerted. "What did Sir Robert want?" he asked in a mollified tone.

"Information had been laid that we were hiding a Jesuit priest."

"Had it, by Jupiter!" He looked at me

closely. "And was it right?" he queried slowly.

"Yes. Francis Hill rode in a few minutes before Sir Robert and his men."

"God's Teeth!" he exclaimed in a whisper and sat down. "What did you do?"

"I put him in the hide behind the cupboard in the Great Hall." His eyes were suddenly sharp and questioning and I hurried on. "I was awakened one night by sounds of carpentry and saw Little John putting the finishing touches to it."

"So — and you've kept it to yourself all these months. At least I know you can keep a secret." He eyed me thoughtfully. "I wonder who hopes for our downfall. Who do you suspect it is . . . that has our welfare at heart?"

I rubbed at a stain on the polished top of the table. "I can only suppose it is my aunt," I told him miserably, intent upon my small task.

"Perhaps — I have news for her which will not be to her liking."

I looked up quickly. "My uncle?"

"Is dead" Conn said baldly. "He was executed for treason a week ago. The Queen was lenient and put the estates in trust for Jane and Dudley . . . but there is a proviso, which your aunt will take exception to. They are to be my wards, under my guardianship, until they are of age in Dudley's case and marry, in Jane's."

I gazed at him speechlessly. "But why has she done this?" I wondered. "How can she grant you such favours, trust you so well . . . ?"

"I told you my father was a friend of King Henry," Conn said roughly and I knew better than to pursue the topic further.

Although I let the matter drop, I could not but wonder at it. By rights Conn should have been suspect, related as he was to a recusant and one involved with the Scottish Queen. Even to myself there seemed enough evidence to implicate him, certainly enough to make the authorities view him with suspicion, and yet he was undisturbed, seeming invulnerable and even given the wardship of my cousins. Turning the matter over in my mind, I recalled other incidents which had seemed of little import at the time, but which now seemed unaccountable. With a sudden chill I remembered the visit of the priest and his errand to meet the man who would arrange a method of communication with the Scottish Queen.

My heart thumped against my tight bodice and I slowly sat down, one hand pressed against my side. All along I had thought my husband in sympathy with the Catholics, but now, I wondered if that was what he wanted people to think and that in fact he was working for the government, one of Walsingham's men that Sir Robert mentioned so often.

Warily trying out this new notion, I realized that it fitted the events very well and explained much that had puzzled me — his seeming invulnerability from arrest, the Queen's consent to our marriage, his absences and the unexpected friendship with Sir Robert — and I could only wonder that it had not occurred to me before.

Conn had ridden over to Hawks' Hill to make known to my aunt the terms of his guardianship. Dudley had chosen to sail with Drake on one of his expeditions in the hope of winning fame and favour, but Jane was to live with us and my husband had control over all my uncle's business ventures and estates. Thinking of my aunt's reactions, I had been relieved when Conn declined my offer to accompany him, but now I was doubly glad of his refusal. With his absence I would have a little time to become accustomed to my new knowledge of his character and by the time he returned would have come to terms with his unexpected role . . . and have decided upon my own reactions.

He returned the next day with Jane riding pillion behind him. One look at her pale, drawn face and I knew how great had been the ordeal for her, and I bore her tenderly away to the comfort and seclusion of the chamber I had prepared for her.

I was unable to speak to Conn alone until some hours later, when we had retired to our bedroom and then I forgot all my carefully prepared speeches and burst out boldly, asking a vital question without delicacy or finesse.

"Are you one of Walsingham's men?"

He stiffened, his hands frozen in the act of unbuttoning his black velvet doublet and stared at me through the blurred reflection of the mirror. After a while his fingers returned to their task, but his eyes were watchful and his attitude alert, like a dog that senses excitement.

"What an extraordinary question," he remarked casually. "What makes you ask it?"

Sitting up in bed I watched his reflection. "Several things have made me wonder — I've always found it odd that the Queen consented to our marriage so readily for one . . . but there were others. One only had to notice them to begin to suspect."

Conn threw the doublet across a chest and turned to me, slim and tall in his black breeches and full white shirt that I had worked myself with fashionable black embroidery.

"What an intelligent little wife," he said softly.

"I daresay you're about to tell me it's none of my business. Whatever you might feel, Conn, it *is* my affair and I would know the truth."

"Too much knowledge is a dangerous thing, Perditta, not only to me, but to all concerned, even you."

He spoke with unusual gravity and looking up, I searched his stern face, knowing I would receive no other answer. "I would ask one question," I said at last. "And for the peace of my mind, pray you to answer it. Did you betray my uncle?"

His hand tightened on the bedcurtain. "No," he answered shortly. "I did not even know he was involved. I had thought him satisfied with being a recusant — refusing to go to church and hiding the visiting priest. I gather his ambition got the better of his discretion and having realized how in favour he'd be if ever Mary came to the throne, he allowed himself to be persuaded to finance the plot."

"I didn't like him, but I'm sorry for him."

He gave a short laugh. "You need not be — he implicated everyone he could think of in an endeavour to save his own skin — even Jane."

178

"Surely not."

"In truth, yes. I'm to keep a very strict control of her. She'll find it hard to find a husband. He'll have to be of unimpeachable loyalty to satisfy the queen."

"She'd make a good wife and mother. Our little Elizabeth loves her already."

"The best she can hope for is a yeoman who has no care for advancing in the world," said Conn, climbing into bed.

I was to remember his words later, but at that moment something else was filling my mind. The mention of my daughter had brought other matters to my remembrance and counting the weeks on my fingers, I was suddenly sure.

"I'm with child again," I announced into the darkness, but Conn only muttered and moved in his sleep and I turned away from him, contemplating this astounding fact that made all the other revelations of the day pall into insignificance.

8

CONN accepted my news with mild interest, nodding as though it were no more than he expected and remarking that it was a good thing that Master Hilliard was arriving soon, while I was still looking my best.

"Motherhood becomes you," he said, eyeing me critically. "You've filled out and bloomed since we have been wed. Master Nicholas Hilliard should enjoy painting you."

"Will he take a likeness of you, too?"

"Do you wish him to?"

I turned away, busying myself with rearranging a bowl of marigolds, saying lightly, "I thought these were to be an investment for our descendants, besides it's only right that the master of Galliard's Hay should hang in his own hall."

There was a silence and I thought that Conn was disappointed with my answer, but could not bring myself to look at him. Since that night in August there had been a constraint between us that grew harder to break with each succeeding day. I missed his companionship, even his teasing would have been welcome, but I found it impossible to make the first move towards reconciliation or even to accept his tentative offers to make amends. Despite the company of Jane and the lively presence of my little Beth (naturally I refused to call her Bess) who even at so young an age showed clearly that she was the possessor of a strong character, I was lonely and tense, hiding my unhappiness behind a brittle, vivacious facade.

The visit of the Court painter was a welcome distraction and I viewed his coming with much interest. He proved to be a handsome, charming man, with the lively, penetrating eyes of a painter.

The first few days he was at Galliard's Hay he spent his time either with my husband or watching me, which at first I found distracting, but once I had become used to his critical examination, I found myself taking more care over my hair or the choice of a gown or jewel. At last he announced himself ready to begin and having asked me to wear my kirtle and bodice of olive green satin, led me to the large mullioned window in the Great Hall and sat me in a pool of sunshine.

Taking a gillyflower from the bowl on the table he asked me to hold it against my bodice and at last satisfied with my position, sat down himself and began to make quick, sure lines on his canvas.

"You have beautiful hands," he remarked, busy with his work. "Much like Her Majesty herself." Suddenly he frowned and his hands grew still as he lifted his eyes from his work to stare at me.

Surprise, recognition and puzzlement followed quickly across his countenance as he openly studied my face.

Has anyone told you that you resemble the Queen?" he asked.

Flattered, I shook my head.

"But surely you must be related? Perhaps the Boleyns are kin to you?" he persisted.

"No," I told him, by this time as puzzled as he.

"But this is astonishing. I've drawn and painted Queen Elizabeth many times and while at first I did not notice the likeness because it was not expected, now that I have seen it, it becomes more and more obvious. I could be sketching the Queen's face. Has no-one else remarked upon it?"

"No and I am sure that Sir Robert Varley, who is about the Court would have done so if it was truly noticeable."

"I find it most interesting. Of course, doubles do occur, but I am sure in this case that there must be common ancestry." He smiled at me and took up his work again. "It might be worth your while to seek it out. High relations can be useful."

"I am sure it must be a chance likeness, nothing more," I told him, warned by some inner sense to make light of the affair, but all the same it proved a good subject to absorb my thoughts while I sat for him.

"Conn," I said that night. "Do I resemble the Queen?"

He considered me, his head a little to one side. "Perhaps. You have the same colouring, but she paints and dyes so much that it's hard to tell what she really looks like behind the image of monarchy she presents."

"Master Hilliard says I do," I went on, taking off my chain of pearls and dropping it in the little wooden box that held my jewels.

"Perhaps you are distantly related to her — it's possible."

"Yes . . . but I don't really know who my kinsfolk are, do I?"

Our eyes met in the mirror, a flare of speculation in both our gazes before Conn stood up abruptly and pulling back the curtains stared out into the garden.

"What we are thinking could be dangerous," he said quietly.

"I know."

He struck the wood of the window frame with his clenched fist and turned back to me with sudden decision. "Is there anyone who knew your parents before you were born — or someone who knew you as a babe?"

I thought. "There's only Dame Bartley. She was a friend of my mother's and knew Aunt Kate. I believe they were young together, but she is very old and might even be dead."

"Do you know where she lives?"

"At Kilver Manor in Somerset."

"I'll go there and make what enquiries I can." Conn looked at me closely. "Are you sure you want to know? You might be the result of a union between a kitchen maid and a scullion!"

I smiled at that. "I'd leifer I was just the daughter of the good people I was brought up to call mother and father," I told him. "If you could prove that I'd be satisfied. After all it might have been malicious lies on the part of my uncle. He would have liked to hurt me."

"I think there is more to it than just Henry Campernowne's wish to be nasty . . . he seemed quite sincere in his belief that you were not his sister's child. Do you think it's possible that your father — ?"

He paused delicately and I shook my head decidedly. "No, my father was not like that. He loved my mother . . . and besides, he was totally involved in his books and studies. He was quite unworldly."

"Human nature has produced many surprises," Conn told me, amusement in his voice.

I wrinkled my nose, feeling more at

ease with him than I had done for some time.

"If you had ever met my father, you would not suggest such a thing," I said and smiled a little at the thought of my tiny, abstracted father, about whom the musty smell of books and papers seemed to cling, being tempted by the delights of the flesh.

As the year of fifteen eighty-six drew towards winter the weather remained fine and the roads passable. Somewhat to my surprise Conn remained firm in his resolution to seek out my mother's girlhood friend and set out on the journey at the end of November.

Master Hilliard had departed, taking the miniature with him in order to set it in a golden case that would hang from a chain and make a delightful and impressive jewel for my husband to wear. I had stared back at the red-haired woman in the miniature with mixed feelings. He had made me attractive certainly, beautiful, Jane said, but the painter had also caught a hint of wary sadness which I did not like others to see. Master Hilliard was altogether too perceptive for my peace of mind.

Christmas approached and by force of circumstances the festive season would not be as happy and carefree as the previous year. Because of the winter gales which kept all ships in harbour, Dudley would be home for the holiday, calling in at Galliard's Hay to collect his sister and take her on with him to Hawks' Hill.

When he rode into the courtyard, I was surprised but not displeased by the changes wrought in him by the happenings of the last few months. Responsibility had given him a new firmness of expression and without the idolatry of his parents he had developed an unexpected strength of character, which showed in his changed demeanour.

"Good morrow, Cousin," he greeted me somewhat gravely, with none of the old boisterous, flamboyant manner.

"I'm glad to see you," I told him and meant it. "We have thought of you, alone in London and with so much upon your shoulders."

"Sir Robert was a great help," he said. "I counted myself lucky to have had his acquaintance."

"I — did not know," I said slowly, "but I am glad you had a good friend."

Jane hurried to greet her brother and I left them alone to exchange confidences while I saw that wine and refreshments were placed on the table.

When it was time for them to go, she turned and hugged me and I patted her shoulder knowing with what apprehension she viewed the coming meeting with her mother.

"I don't like to leave you," she said tremulously. "Little Beth will hardly know me when I return."

"Nonsense," I told her, speaking bracingly. "Conn and I will come for you on Twelfth Day and bring you home with us." I looked meaningly over her shoulder at her brother. "I'm sure you need have no fear, Dudley will let no-one bully you or treat you unkindly."

I saw him start and smiled a little to realize that until that moment, he had been quite oblivious of his parents' ill treatment of his sister. However, he answered almost at once, speaking stoutly.

"Indeed, sweet sis, I give you my word

that no one will treat you with less than the kindness you deserve."

Giving her a quick kiss I pushed her towards him. "On your way then, while there's still time to reach Hawks' Hill before dusk. We'll come for you, never fear. Remember your mother has invited us to join you for the last night of Christmas."

Still she hesitated. "I don't like leaving you — "

"Conn will be home soon," I assured myself as much as Cousin Jane and followed them to the door, waving until they were lost to view and I could return to my comfortable parlour and worry about my husband, while I sewed a small gown for Beth and the burning logs sent showers of sparks up the wide chimney.

My husband had intended to be gone a little over a week, but already nine days had elapsed since his departure and with each succeeding day I was growing a little more worried, especially since the weather which had been good for so long, showed signs of turning cold. Opening the curtains of my bedchamber that night, I looked out at the glittering, frost-covered scene and shivered a little. As my frozen feet sought the comfort of the brick which had been heated in the kitchen oven and placed to warm the bed, I found myself praying for his safe return and realizing what I was doing, was somewhat puzzled by my action.

Conn rode in the next day, confounding my fears and filling me with relief at his return.

I returned his greeting more fervently than of late and his glance was a little questioning as he seated himself in his chair beside the fire.

"Dudley has taken Jane to Hawks' Hill and besides, I want to know if you have found out anything of import."

Conn leaned back and laughed at my lame defense. "So — you are merely feeling lonely and curious, when I thought you were glad to have me home."

I looked down at the toes of my shoes peeping out from the edge of my full skirt. "That too," I admitted shyly and could not keep the hot colour from staining my cheeks.

Without a word, Conn stretched his

hand to me and when I placed mine within his grasp, drew me to sit on a low stool at his feet.

"How's young Elizabeth?" he asked lazily, stretching his long legs to the fire, relaxing as he sipped the wine I had heated to warm him.

I answered readily and for a while our conversation centered on the doings of the prodigy who ruled our nursery. I leaned against Conn's thigh while he played idly with the wisps of hair that escaped the confines of my lace cap and a feeling of peace crept over me as we talked and the fire crackled an accompaniment.

"It's a pity I did not set out sooner for I found a house of mourning," my husband said at last, returning to the reason for his journey.

I twisted round to look up at him with dismay and would have asked eager questions, but he shook his head and put a finger on my lips.

"Let me speak, wife. Dame Bartley was lately dead and newly laid to rest in her grave. However, the family treated me kindly and once they knew my errand which I presented as nothing more than a desire on your part to learn about your mother's youth, were most eager to help. Indeed, so assiduous were they in recalling the names and whereabouts of any who might prove of use that it was more than a week later before I could make my escape."

He rose to refill our goblets, before settling back as before and resuming his tale.

"Most of the people had removed themselves or died but at last I found one aged crone who had been nurse to Dame Bartley's own children. Like most servants she proved to know a great deal about the family she served and had I wished to hear gossip and scandal about long gone Bartleys I would still have been there." He caught my impatient eye and paused tantalisingly.

"Oh, *Conn*!" I wailed and seeing my very real agitation, he ceased to tease and went on.

"The old nurse had lost her teeth, but not her wits and remembered your mother and Mistress Kate. When she knew who I was and after I had clinked my purse meaningly once or twice she was prepared to tell me all she knew — which I'm afraid was not much. She confirmed that your mother was thought by all to be past the age of childbearing and she seemed vague about where you had been born, saying that your parents had been away and they returned bringing you with them. I gathered the event was a nine-days wonder and for a while your mother bore the nickname of 'Sarah'."

I was unable to hide my disappointment. "And that's all?"

"Almost. She did say that she heard that Master and Mistress Fox had joined the Queen on part of her progress that summer."

I looked up quickly, but Conn shook his head.

"Don't retain too much hope upon it, Perditta. If your mother was, indeed, whom we suspect, then the trail would be well covered. I fear you must resign yourself to the fact that you will never know for certain."

"But it all fits," I cried eagerly. "My mother being Kate Ashley's cousin, they were both Campernowne's, you know.

My hair and the resemblance Nicholas Hilliard noticed. The Queen being my Godparent . . . the money my father left me — and now we know they were on a progress together when I was born."

Conn looked at me, his face grave in the flickering light from the fire. "Take my advice, wife," he said, his voice sober, "and keep these thoughts to yourself. If word got abroad it would be accounted treason and we could well end in the Tower."

I shivered and grew silent and after a while Conn fell to playing with my hair again.

"Cannot you be satisfied with being yourself?" he asked.

"I was satisfied to be my parents' child until Henry Campernowne raised all manner of doubts in my mind. Now I want with all my heart to know who were in truth my parents."

"I fear you may never know."

"I shall wonder all my life."

He touched my lips lightly with his finger. "Wonder by all means, but to yourself. Let none of this pass your lips save to me. These suppositions must be ours alone, no-one else must ever have an inkling of your suspicions."

I sighed and put such thoughts aside for the time being. Soon household events claimed me; Christmas was upon us, with all its attendant tasks and the proposed visit to Hawks' Hill, to be looked forward to with apprehension, approached with more speed than I cared for.

The weather was still cold, but dry and with no sign of snow so, leaving Beth in the care of her nurse, we rode over on a single horse, myself riding pillion behind Conn, for warmth and safety.

My aunt greeted us coldly with no pretence of pleasure, but Jane and Dudley were obviously pleased to see us, but it was the woman in a rich, red gown, turning round from the fire that made me tingle with surprise.

"Good morrow — may I give you the season's greetings?" said Bess Death, dropping into so low a curtsey that my husband was bound to give her his hand to raise her.

"Master Death was wondering only the other day when it was he would see you, Sir Conn," she pouted, tapping him playfully on the sleeve. "I vow at one time we saw you so often, we quite thought of you as one of the family."

"I'm flattered," he said quietly, "but must remind you that I am a family man now and with less time to spare for other things."

She smiled up at him, her black eyes sparkling and looking so provoking and beautiful that I could willingly have pushed her into the fire.

"I doubt not that you're aware that I am a mother myself. I have the sweetest little boy. Ashley is so dark and handsome, he quite fills my heart with joy to look at him, but then I've always had a preference for dark men."

Conn threw me a speaking glance so full of entreaty that my anger dissolved into amusement and I hurried to his aid, knowing beyond any doubt that whatever he had once felt for Mistress Death, now she caused him no other feelings than embarrassment, a feeling most deadly to affection.

"Why, Mistress Death," I said, skirting my husband's tall figure and warming my hands at the fire, "may I compliment you upon your gown? In a few years' time I hope to make use of just such a colour myself. I've often heard how becoming a warm shade is when one is past one's youth."

She looked at me in astonishment, her eyes wide and her mouth still set in the sweet simper with which she had thought to ensnare Conn anew. I almost laughed at her surprise at my rudeness, but before I could speak, her expression changed swiftly to one of rage, her face losing its attraction and becoming ugly and hard.

"Why, Lady Galliard," she hissed, her voice shrill and penetrating, "the gossip's gone around that you've had unwelcome visitors at Galliard's Hay. How I feel for you and hope that the affair didn't prove too distressing."

"Your hope was fulfilled," said Conn's voice over my shoulder, his tone so cold that I knew he must have realized the implications of her speech as well as I. "Sir Robert Varley is a family friend," he went on. "Whoever thought to lay false information against us should have made sure of his facts before sending him upon a wasted errand."

Reading his expression, she gave a stifled exclamation of suppressed anger and turned away abruptly, leaving us with an agitated rustle of petticoats.

"I thought it was my aunt," I murmured. "I feel I owe her an apology."

"She wouldn't thank you for it — " He looked down at me, searching my face. "You must believe that I had no idea she would be here," he said.

"No more had I, or I wouldn't have come. I have no liking for Mistress Death," I told him, so candidly that he smiled and carried my hand to his mouth.

His lips touched my palm in an intimate gesture and for a moment I was uncomfortably reminded of my last meeting with Sir Robert, but quickly pushed the treacherous thought aside and allowed Conn to slide his arm round my waist as he led me to join a group of local gentry talking together in a far corner of the room.

The weather seemed only to have been waiting for Christmas to be over before it changed and January saw snow filled valleys and impassable roads. We were snug enough in Galliard's Hay and apart from chapped fingers and chilblained toes, knew little discomfort, the outside world seeming of little importance in our secure, insular existence, but with February came the thaw and news which shook our cosy society to its foundations.

By the end of the month we knew that Mary, Queen of Scots had been executed at Fotheringhay and that Her Majesty, having disdained all involvement, had banished her Secretary of State, Lord Burghley, for managing the matter so expediently.

For a while we talked of the affair in hushed voices, Jane and I admitting to compassion for the imprisoned queen, but Conn holding that it should have taken place years ago. With the better weather came the departure of Dudley and homely events assumed greater importance than those that involved unknown people. Jane and I busied ourselves with packing his chest with whatever we thought would give him comfort on his voyage with Sir Francis Drake and tucked away thick knitted sea-socks and pots of preserve to remind him of home.

Jane clung to him at the door and I saw tears glittering in her eyes as he rode away.

"He'll be back with a chestful of Spanish treasure," I comforted her, but she shook head.

"I have a feeling that something will happen to him," she said sadly and went away to comfort herself by cuddling my daughter.

During the previous autumn we had heard rumours of a great fleet of ships being gathered together by the King of Spain with the intention of invading England and for the first time we heard the word 'Armada,' which we were all soon to know so well and which was to strike dread into our hearts for so many months. Then came news that Sir Francis Drake was setting out to demolish this 'Armada' in its very harbour and remembering Jane's premonition I prayed for Dudley's safety while his sister grew pale and silent.

Seeing our anxiety, Conn sent into Alton for a news sheet, and poring over the rough paper and bad print we learned that the expedition had been a complete success and that we were safe from attack for the remainder of that year at least, while the Spaniards made good their losses. Despite the good news, Jane remained unconvinced and at last came word from Hawks' Hill that confirmed her feelings; Dudley's ship had lost touch with Drake's fleet while involved in the fight at Cadiz and no news of her had been heard since.

"It's early yet — she could have been disabled and be making her way slowly home. The sea is so vast it could take months . . . don't despair yet, Jane."

She tried to smile at my attempt to comfort her, but I knew that in her heart she was certain that her brother was dead. It saddened me to see her so unhappy and I longed for my baby to be born, hoping that it would fill the gap in her heart.

At last my babe made it known that she was impatient to be born and arrived early one morning in June. Conn hid his feelings at being presented with another daughter, but I knew he must be disappointed and wondered myself if all the effort was worth this puny, little mortal, until I held her in my arms and she gazed at me blankly with Conn's dark eyes. Love for the tiny scrap of humanity I had created flowed over me and from that moment I never ceased to give thanks for my two daughters.

Catherine, as she was christened, was much smaller than Beth, who had always been a bonny child. With one so dark and pale and the other red-haired and pink complexioned, there never were sisters so different and the servants called them Rose Red and Snow White after the old fairytale.

Despite the missing Dudley, that early part of the summer seemed filled with joy and contentment. It was not so much that we forgot him, or grieved less for him, but that our lives were filled by the needs of the children, who took up every minute of our time. After so many uneasy months, worrying over the Armada invasion or Catholic plots and the dangers of visiting priests, suddenly there appeared nothing to disturb our calm — the future stretched ahead peaceful and secure.

During the last few months a few houses for our workers had been built a short way from our gates and each time I saw them I could not but admire their workmanship. Conn had employed a carpenter to cut the framework and roof timbers, but the families themselves had filled the walls and set a cap of thatch over all. Curls of smoke rose from their red brick chimneys and already flowers and vegetables had been planted against their walls by the more industrious.

Usually when I rode through the inhabitants called respectful greetings to me, touching their forelock or bobbing curtseys and I had grown to expect such salutes, which made it surprising when I received no such respects one morning towards the end of August.

Upon closer inspection the entire site seemed deserted; no children played beside the houses and every shutter was tightly closed, only the thin drifts of smoke told of anyone at home.

"Where is everyone?" I asked the groom who had accompanied me and was as puzzled as I.

He shifted uneasily in his saddle, turning to look about him with growing apprehension. "I don't like it, Mistress — "

he began, when a whimper carried clearly to our ears.

Looking for its cause, I set my mare into motion, urging her slowly forward, while my eyes searched the dusty track between the houses. Coming upon what looked like a small bundle of rags, I edged my mount towards it, approaching carefully until I could identify the object, flinging myself from the saddle as I realized a young child lay there.

As I bent to touch it, a shutter behind me was flung open and an anxious voice shouted from the dark interior. "Don't touch it, Mistress."

I paused with my hand outstretched. "There's nothing to fear — it's a child. A sick one by the look."

"Sick, aye — it's smallpox."

Horror shook me that the disease we all feared should have found its way to Galliard's Hay and catching my breath I drew back, my knees weak and trembling.

"How did it get here — it couldn't have walked?"

"The mother brought it, afore she died. We got hooks and dragged her away, but the child's not dead yet."

I was struck by the callous action, but knowing the death toll of the dreadful illness could not condemn the villagers. As I glanced fearfully down at the bundle at my feet a thin, stick-like arm waved feebly and a soft cry, more a moan than a sob came to me, touching me to pity. Dragging a corner of my petticoat across my mouth, I knelt beside the child.

"Have sense, Mistress!" called the voice from the house. "Tis only a pauper's brat, not fit to live and soon dead if we leave it there."

"Pauper it might be, but no less a human for all that and no less deserving of compassion," I said roundly and reached to uncover the child, with hands that shook with fear.

As soon as I saw the poor, little sore-encrusted face, red and flushed with fever, my fear left me and I knew that I could not ignore his cry for help. Even if he died within a few hours, I would, for my own conscience, have to do my best to comfort him and ease his last hours.

"Ned," I called to the groom, who had retreated to a safe distance. "Do you ride home and tell Mistress Jane what has happened. Say that I shall take the child to the hut made ready for lambing — she'll know what I will need."

Ignoring the disapproving murmur from behind the windows, I lifted the boy in my arms and rose carefully. The child, who appeared about two years old, weighed no more than Beth and I carried him easily. The lambing hut was in a field, far enough away from Galliard's Hay to prevent infection. By the time I reached it, Jane had made it ready and I found water and herbs as well as linen and cooling drinks.

I cried over the thin little body as I washed it. Before wrapping him in a piece of linen, I laid him on a bed of straw. In health the child must have been pretty and thinking of my own children, I prayed for the soul of his mother who had carried him so far. Scabs caked his mouth, but I soaked a rag in wine and water and squeezed a few drops between his parched lips. From the first I knew it was a hopeless task and just before noon he died. I like to think I comforted him a little — I hope I did.

I waved from the door of the hut and a servant who had been waiting approached cautiously.

"Bring me a cloak and have a bath made ready in my chamber. Then set fire to the hut," I told him and as he left, turned back to say a last prayer for the unknown child.

The doorway behind me darkened and I turned to see Conn, who had been away from home, holding a cloak.

"What foolishness is this?" he demanded.

"I could not leave him to die in the road like an animal," I said, realizing his anger arose from anxiety.

"Come away quickly," he urged. "Take off your clothes and leave them to be burned."

I stripped off my garments and as I stepped out of the hut, Conn wrapped the cloak around me. I had left even my shoes behind and he picked me up and carried me to the house as the servants ran across the field with sticks and tinder. Glancing back I saw a flame leap and with incredible speed the wooden hut was enveloped in fire.

"Pray God, that's an end to it," muttered Conn and hurrying up the stairs, I echoed his prayer.

9

NO-ONE knows how the illness is spread, the only sure thing is that it takes all alike, leaping from person to person with deadly speed, striking a whole family within hours. It is unpredictable in choosing its victims, seeming to take old or young, strong or weak with equal greed.

Conn sent Jane away, and declaring that having taken cowpox as a child he was immune to small-pox, took my care upon himself, making me scour myself from head to toe with hot water and pungent herbs until I was red and almost raw.

"God grant you are safe", he said, emotion making his voice gruff. "How you could endanger yourself — and perhaps bring the infection home to the children — " In his agitation he seized my shoulders and shook me.

"It was something I *had* to do. *You* could not have left him there."

"No, but I am not likely to take it. Milkmaids are known not to catch the illness and as a child I was put among them to take the lesser cowpox."

"I'll keep away from the babes — and if you wish sleep elsewhere."

He caught me up and kissed me roughly for answer and I spoke no more about taking my bed to another chamber.

At first I was anxious, expecting every minute to be smitten down, but as the days went by I grew confident that I had escaped the contagion and, while not venturing near my daughters, dared to hover in the doorway of their nursery and gaze my fill at them.

Almost three weeks had passed and when I developed a headache, I did not at first connect it with the pox, but put it down to an approaching thunderstorm. But when I developed violent shivers and discovered a fleeting rash on my body — a sign I knew of small pox, I bolted my door and would let no-one enter.

By the time Conn rattled the latch, I could hardly drag myself across the room to open the door and had only a hazy memory of being carried back to bed.

"Oh, Conn," I wailed against his neck, "I don't want to die!"

"Be sure I won't let you," he answered and I carried his determined voice down with me as I plunged into a vortex of pain and fever induced dreams and nightmares so terrible that I screamed aloud and fought the hands that held me in the bed in my wild desire to escape.

Of the first days I have no memory at all and even after that the recollection is hazy. Later I discovered that Conn nursed me himself, caring for me, sponging my body that burned with fever with cooling water and fighting for my life with every ounce of his determination. I remember waking dreamily one night, to see his dim outline silhouetted in the moonlight from the window. He rose at once as I turned my head, his own movements so weary and tired that I was anxious on his behalf.

I tried to tell him to rest, to go to sleep, but the sound I made was no stronger or more intelligible than that of a new babe and he held a drink to my lips, laying a hand on my forehead as he put me back against the pillows.

"You'll do, wife," I heard him say, a triumphant note in his voice for all his fatigue. "The fever's broke."

The next time I awoke it was daylight and Conn was sitting on the windowseat, reading. For a while I lay there watching him, noting the new lines on his face and the deep shadows under his eyes, before he felt my regard and looked up. At once his face was alive and there was the familiar, wicked smile on his lips.

"We beat it, sweetheart," he said, dropping his book and crossing swiftly to the bed. "We sent old Death apacking, you and I."

"The children?" I managed to croak weakly.

"Well — never better. No-one else took the disease. Sleep now and get your strength back."

I moved my hand and realizing my wish he took it in his own firm grasp. Exerting all my strength I gave a slight tug and he bent nearer to catch my words.

"Lie with me," I whispered.

He understood at once and climbing on

to the bed beside me, gathered me into his arms, cradling my head on his shoulder. I sighed with content and nestled closer, realizing by his breathing that exhaustion had overcome his strength and that he had fallen asleep. For a while I fought to keep my eyes open while I made a silent prayer of thankfulness, but sleep tugged at my eyelids and within a few seconds I, too, was asleep.

A few days later I was enough aware of myself and my surroundings to make a discovery. I had reached up to smooth my hair and where there should have been long strands my hand encountered short, spiky tufts.

"My hair!" I cried.

"I cut it off during your fever," Conn explained.

I stared up at him, tears welling in my eyes. "My one beauty," I whispered, in my weakness unable to accept this trifling blow.

"What a vain wretch!" exclaimed Conn. "Saved but this instant from death and already worrying about your looks." He studied me, his head on one side. "To tell the truth, you look rather engaging . . . unusual enough to be attractive."

I looked at him, unable to curb my curiosity even the while I knew he was teasing me. "How so?" I asked.

Conn smiled, his eyes gleaming and I was pleased that he felt I was well enough to be chaffed.

"Somewhat in resemblance to a new born chick," he said and lest I be hurt, bent to kiss me.

I chuckled at the picture his words presented and at the sound of my mirth, he laughed aloud, the joyous sound filling the room. We laughed until the tears filled our eyes and then weakly we sat and beamed at each other, grinning inanely with the liberation from weeks of anxiety.

I recovered slowly, surprised to discover how thin and weak I had become, scarcely recognizing the woman who looked back at me from my mirror. Luckily my scars were slight and would soon fade. As soon as we judged the infection well past, the children were brought to my room and I was amazed to see how they had grown in the weeks since I had seen them. Beth was over a year old and doing her best to walk, while Kate, as Catherine had become, at nearly four months had progressed into knowingness, her eyes alert with an intelligence beyond her age.

Jane said, "Beth has missed you," as she put her on my bed and the babe tottered into my arms.

"I must thank you for your care of them."

"It did me good," she answered simply. "I was immersed in my own sorrow. With the babies dependant upon me, I had no time to think."

I was ashamed to realize I had completely forgotten about the loss of her brother and asked quickly if there had been any news.

Sadly she shook her head and seeing how her eyes followed my children, I wished her married with babes of her own to love. With this in mind I spoke to Conn later.

"We should find her a husband — after all as her guardian you have a duty to see her settled. Have you no eligible friends we could invite to visit us?"

"How about Robert Varley?" he asked,

after some thought. "Unless he's yearning after some married woman, it's time he took a wife."

I looked at him quickly, wondering if he suspected the unfulfilled relationship between myself and Sir Robert, but he appeared intent upon picking fluff from his velvet doublet and did not look up.

"I don't know," I said slowly, at last. "He is used to a courtier's life and Jane is totally unused to such things."

"I invited him to stay some time ago," said Conn, "and if they are not adverse, perhaps something can be arranged. After all you and I, Perditta, had no love match when we were wed . . . and yet I believe we deal well together."

I knew then that he either realized or suspected my feelings for the other man and that with his usual arbitrary attitude to others, this was his way of settling the matter.

"Has anyone ever named you despot?" I asked, irritated by his complacency.

"Not to my face," he told me, cheerfully. "In this case, you'll see I'm right. I know all the people concerned and have their welfare at heart."

He was gone before I could tell him that I had no wish to have Sir Robert as a house guest and I lay against my pillows, listening to the clatter of his boots on the stairs and pondering upon his action. Knowing Conn as well as I did I knew there must be more behind his suggestion that Jane should marry Sir Robert than at first appeared and was more than a little puzzled by his apparent wish to present the Queen's man with an opportunity for dalliance.

I was on my feet again and just taking the strings of the household back into my hands when word came of another Armada threat and by October all our ships were put on orders to 'stand by' and be ready to set sail at a moment's notice. This filled our minds and our conversations until Christmas approached once more and occupied our hands and thoughts with more mundane matters. Glad to have something else to think about, Jane and I flung ourselves into an orgy of work.

For appearance's sake my Aunt Campernowne had accepted our invitation to spend the twelve days of Christmas with us and the Summers from nearby Summer Ho were to be houseguests. I hoped their presence in the house would ease Sir Robert's visit and found myself not looking forward to meeting the Queen's man again, a happening which I viewed both with embarrassment and apprehension.

However, when he finally arrived and I gave him my hand as I sank into a welcoming curtsey, I found that I need not have been bothered at all; whatever my suspicions, there appeared no constraint between the courtier and my husband. Indeed there was an air of wary friendship clinging to them and the relief as I rose and met Sir Robert's eyes was unimaginable, the smile he gave me so kind and full of understanding that I knew I had nothing to fear.

He kissed me lightly in greeting and then turned and saluted Jane in the same way.

"We are flattered that you could leave the joys of London to celebrate the festive season in deepest Hampshire," I said.

"I count myself richer for being invited," he answered. "You must know that this part of the country holds my heart."

The words were for my ears alone, but I looked around quickly to see that Conn was nowhere near, saying brightly and over-loudly, "The Master and Mistress of Summer Ho are spending the holiday with us. You must know them for Dame Allis is one of the Queen's Ladies." I nodded in the couple's direction.

"Everyone knows Dame Allis," Robert told me. "She has a tongue and wit not unlike her royal mistress, which comes, I doubt not, from spending so many hours together."

"I like her."

"That I can well believe — you are two of a kind."

For a while longer we talked of trivialities, of my illness, of his career . . . of the children, the situation with Spain, until others claimed us and we drifted apart, but many times that evening our glances met across the room and I knew that we must contrive a way of meeting.

The opportunity came the next day. The weather was fine and tempted by the pale, winter sunshine the company had mounted horses and ventured out of the warm confines of Galliard's Hay in search of exercise. Noting that Sir Robert kept close, I hung back letting the others ride ahead and waiting for the right moment slipped into a coppice, certain that he would follow.

Once in the shelter of the bare branches, the Queen's man dismounted and came to my side. Sliding from my saddle I fell into his embrace, feeling his arms enclose me, as our thick, winter cloaks fell about us in warm enveloping folds.

We kissed, our lips cold in the chill air, our breath white puffs of steam against the bleak, frosty surroundings.

At last I broke away, putting both hands against his chest to hold him off. "He knows — I'm sure Conn knows," I said.

"You know why I am here?"

Looking down, I nodded. "To see if Jane would suit you as a wife."

"I need to marry, sweeting," he said softly. "I grow no younger and of late have found myself viewing the sons of others with envy."

"Of course — I understand that, but *Jane*? You'd be so near, an ever present hurt. I cannot understand why Conn should even suggest it."

"Perhaps, he thinks we'd grow less fond of each other or more likely he knows that my honour would not allow an affair with a friend's wife."

I looked up, knowing that he had found the real reason behind my husband's actions and gently released myself. "I believe you have it," I said wearily. "How clever he is. He's won and so easily — neither of us can ever put up a fight."

A tear slid down my cheek and I brushed it impatiently away, turning blindly to search for my horse's reins.

Hands took the tangle from my cold fingers and shook out the knot.

"He's — good to you?" asked Sir Robert, intently examining the smooth strips of leather he held.

"Oh, yes. He cared for me himself when I had the smallpox. He had my portrait painted by Master Hilliard and wears my likeness in a jewel about his neck, he teases me and treats me like a wife, which might pass for affection in another man, but I feel I am a possession to be watched over and cared for, but never loved."

Sir Robert looked at me gravely. "Some people find it hard to show their feelings," he said. "I may be wrong, but I think that Conn cares for you greatly."

Too astonished to speak, I allowed him to help me back into the saddle and we cantered out of the wood, joining the others as they rode back, certain that we had not been missed.

I was wrong in this surmise, but was not to learn this until some hours later. We had all sat up late, playing cards and talking, while the men drew on long pipes and filled the air with smoke. At last our guests yawned mightily and declared themselves ready for bed. It had been a struggle to keep my eyes open for the last halfhour and it was with relief that I lighted them to their bedchambers.

Conn followed me into our room and jerking his head to the waiting maid, closed the door behind her. I watched him a little uneasily in the mirror as I

222

took off the queen's pearls and laid them in their box.

He came up behind me, his reflection dim in the light of the candles, the thick, silver chain of the Hilliard jewel that hung from his shoulders gleaming against the dark velvet of his doublet. Unable to meet his gaze, I busied myself unpinning my lace ruff, until he reached out and covered my fingers with his hand.

"Did you enjoy your 'tête a tête' this morning?"

I grew still, feeling a pulse flutter in my throat and taking my shoulders Conn turned me, unresisting, to face him. Fingers pushed up my chin and against my will I was forced to meet his eyes.

"Did you think I didn't notice?" He laughed a little.

"You planned it all," I accused.

"Of course I'm not sure about you, Perditta, but I'd wager that Sir Robert has a well developed sense of honour. I'd stake my fortune that he would never seduce the wife of a friend and even less the wife of a kinsman."

"You aren't related yet," was all I

could think of to say.

"He told me this evening that he intends to approach your cousin tomorrow."

"And if she refuses his offer?"

"She would hardly be so foolish. To spurn the chance of a home of her own would be an act of stupidity and one that I believe Jane Campernowne too sensible to take. No, my dear, she'll take him."

"You'll not force her?"

"I'll have no need. Take my word for it, she'll be willing if not eager."

I suspected he was right, but had to be sure and sought out my cousin the next day as soon as I could be sure with any certainty that Robert had spoken to her. I found her in the nursery, sitting by the fire, nursing the baby on her lap, her face introspective and thoughtful.

I went to her at once and put my hand on her shoulder, nodding dismissal to the hovering maid.

Jane carefully retied Kate's bonnet strings, speaking with her head bowed, apparently intent upon her task.

"Sir Robert has asked me to marry him," she said quietly.

"I know . . . Will you accept him?"

"I think so." She wiped the dribble from Kate's mouth and gave her a silver teething ring to bite on.

Suddenly I took the babe from her and replaced her in her cradle, then sitting beside my cousin I took her hands in mine.

"Jane," I said earnestly, "don't marry him just for a home — you are always more than welcome here."

"Dear Perditta." She smiled and pressed my hands. "Sir Robert is . . . attractive and no doubt reasonable. I believe I could become quite fond of him."

"But is that enough?"

She looked at me gravely. "Many have married with less," she pointed out. "Yourself for one."

I released her hands and looked away.

"Forgive me for asking, but I've often wondered if you and Conn were happy?"

"He regards me as a chattel," I answered and heard the bitterness in my voice.

"But — he cared for you so attentively when you fell ill of the smallpox — "

"Because he disliked the thought of

losing anything which he regarded as belonging to him, not because he was . . . fond of me. Have you ever looked at his crest and motto?" I asked suddenly, hurrying on before she could reply. "Surely you must have noticed it. It's carved over the fireplace in the Great Hall — a clenched, mailed fist and the words 'What I have I hold.' I suppose they belong to Conn's family, but they could have been applied to him."

Jane stared at me. "I had no idea," she murmured. "I envied you your husband and home . . . and babies. I did not realize that you were unhappy."

I stood up and took an impatient turn about the room, my skirt swinging over my farthingale.

"I know many would envy me," I said at last, "and I suppose I should be grateful, but Conn is so — tyrannical, so arbitrary. He never thinks of others. If only he would say, just once, that he loves me . . . "

"Ah," said Jane as though I had explained all to her. "Do you love him?"

"Of course not!" I said quickly. "I owe

him a certain affection which is due to my husband. *Love*, my dear Jane, is reserved for old romances."

She looked wise, but let the subject drop, and after a while I picked up Beth who had toddled to my knee and kissed her smooth, red hair. Jane smiled down at the sleeping baby and took her foot from the rocker.

"I hope I have just such a pair," she said.

I hugged Beth closer. "I love them dearly, but I hope for a boy next time."

"Are you — ?"

I shook my head. "No — but I doubt not that I soon will be." I gave my daughter the keys that hung at my waist to play with and glanced across at the other woman. "Do you intend to take Sir Robert?"

"Yes," she answered simply and I knew that her decision was made.

I knew that the Queen's man would make a good husband and that my sweet Jane deserved such a one, but even so could not still the pang of jealousy that bit at my heart; once wed I knew Robert Varley would be for ever denied to me. While he was my perfect gentle knight and would remain so in my mind, Conn's earthly vigour called to my spirit and Jane's probing had made me realize that over the years I had grown to care for him more than I suspected. I was suddenly surprised to feel the intensity with which I longed for his love — not just the casual affection which he bestowed on anything he owned, but something that would be mine alone.

As though they were lovers eager to avoid delay, Jane and Robert Varley were married as soon as could be arranged after Christmas, waiting only for permission from his Royal mistress before setting the date. While Jane and I and the maids sewed the bride clothes, the men and their lawyer sat over the weighty business of the marriage documents.

I was amused by Conn's insistence. "*We* had no such things when we were wed," I reminded him.

"There was no need," he answered. "I knew what I was worth and that I had no urgent desire to prop up my ailing fortune with your inheritance."

"But surely neither has Sir Robert."

"I'm Jane's guardian and as such it's my duty to see her settled well," Conn said stubbornly. "My man of business will tie them up so well that I can relinquish my role without a qualm — after all your cousin's heiress to a sizeable fortune."

I sighed. "Poor Dudley. It's a year now since he was here. I suppose there's no hope for him now."

"I've had a man enquiring at the harbours, but there's no news of his ship. None of the sailors he questioned had heard of her — she seems to have vanished without a trace."

"I did not know you had made enquiries."

Conn gave me a straight look at the note of surprise I was unable to suppress. "I am neither so hard nor so indifferent as you suppose me," he said, his own voice dry. "You might give me benefit for some understanding where my family is concerned . . . I am no harsh, unfeeling monster, you know."

"Then, marriage has mellowed you," I told him, matching his voice, but inwardly I wondered not a little. For the first time since I had known him,

Conn had admitted to a softer side to his nature, where once he would have heartily refuted any need for a gentler facet to his strong character.

Foregoing my usual rusts and greens, I had chosen violet velvet for the main dress, opening to show an underskirt of satin in a softer shade, with wide, slashed sleeves embroidered with pearls, and felt that I would rival any Court lady in such a gown at Jane's wedding. Jane's gown was rosepink, and seeing us in our finery, Conn waxed poetical, declaring that we reminded him of nothing so much as a posy from the garden.

The guests were to gather at the church, before coming on to the celebrations which were to be held at Galliard's Hay and a few days later the bridal pair would leave to take up residence at Hawks' Hill, where they would make their home.

Conn had engaged some musicians and the Great Hall was a lively scene that evening, the stately rows of dancers resembling rainbows as they leapt and swayed in time to drums and flute.

I must confess that my heart pained me a little as Robert led out Jane for the first dance, and knowing the emotion that the courtier and I shared I could not but wonder what hope they had for happiness. Watching them together I knew that Robert's natural kindness and courtesy would prevent his ever hinting that his love was elsewhere and could see that Jane's diffidence and pretty shyness had already attracted his chivalry. The course of the dance brought them face to face and as they paused, posturing gracefully, Jane slowly raised her head, her eyes seeking Sir Robert's.

Reading the glances they exchanged I grew weak with relief. Desiring above all the happiness of these two people so special to me, I knew beyond doubt that they had established the beginnings of a concord that by God's grace would last them through life; neither had the character to sustain the wild emotions of a passionate love, but I hoped and believed that their quiet affection would be none the worse for that.

I had been leaning over the balustrade, looking down into the Great Hall intent upon the scene below, when suddenly I grew aware that someone was watching from the shadows behind me and I turned uneasily, feeling the hair stand up on the back of my neck.

As I stared into the gloom beyond the flickering light cast by the candles, I could dimly make out the shape of a man leaning against the far wall, his arms folded and one leg crossed over the other as he watched me, his short cloak a pool of darkness behind him.

"It's far distant to our wedding day," said Conn, nodding to the throng below. "Are you envious that you watch so intently?"

I considered, turning back to look down at the colourful crowd, the murmuring of their voices rising above the music. "I was watching Jane and Robert — and hoping that life will be kind to them, but I don't envy them their marriage rites. Such a conventional beginning would hardly have suited us . . . not every bride is forcibly wed, abducted and taken to live in a half-finished house!"

Conn came closer, his mulberry velvet taking colour from the candles. "Would you have it different, Perditta?" he asked, his voice a deep breath of sound.

I searched his face which was rendered inscrutable by the deep shadows, only his eyes catching what light there was and gleaming in his dark countenance. "No," I whispered at last.

"No more would I," he answered and I knew that for all his commonplace words, for the first time he had come near to telling me he cared for me.

10

THE year of 1588 opened with portents of gloom and ill tidings. Countrywide wisemen and astronomers prophesied destruction and doom. Even in Galliard's Hay we were not immune from the general malaise as I found out one afternoon in early April.

I had ridden out to take a recipe for a concoction to whiten the skin to Dame Allis at Summer Ho; my mother's book had proved invaluable for such things and I was rapidly gaining a reputation for my ointments and cordials. Having delivered my recipe, I spent some time gossiping and listening to her tales of court life, which I may say gave me room for thought and made me view Sir Robert with quite different eyes. If her stories were true, then he could hardly be the innocent I had supposed. I took my leave and set out to return home, forsaking the road and taking a track through the woods for speed.

So intent was I on the thoughts induced by Allis Summer's tales that I would have ridden by the rough hut without noticing it, but for the fact that the pungent smell of smoke had wafted to my nostrils and made me slow my horse and look about.

The tiny shelter was made out of the most primitive materials, branches and twigs covered by a layer of thick mud and topped by a course thatch of heather. A fire burned outside the low door and an aged woman stirred the contents of a large, black cooking pot that hung over it from the apex of three branches bound together to form a triangle.

The old woman heard our hooves and looked up, holding her iron ladle like a weapon, her stance wary and watchful.

"Come away, mistress," urged the groom, who had dropped behind me. "'Tis old Grannie Green and best left alone."

Taking no notice of his obvious unease, I rode forward and leaning in my saddle looked down at the woman, taking in her tattered clothes and wrinkled face.

"Give me Good Morrow," I said politely. "You have chosen a good site for your home."

She looked round the glade, formed by a dip in the land and sheltered on all sides by the surrounding trees and nodded.

"Aye," she agreed. "It's a good place."

"Have you lived here long — I haven't seen you before?"

"Long enough," she answered succinctly. "I know who you be, lady, for all you've not seen me afore. You're the mistress of the big house over yonder. You've had both the smallpox and a wedding this last year."

"Everyone who lives nearby could tell me that and not think themselves clever," I retorted.

"Aye — but how many could tell you about a golden haired lad who sailed away?"

She paused invitingly and I stared down at her, my eyes narrowed as I calculated the likelihood of her having heard of Dudley's loss from one of my household.

"It's no secret," I said shortly and

236

gathered up my reins preparing to move on.

A claw-like brown hand reached up to hold my bridle, the black grimed nails filling me with revulsion. Behind me my groom started forward and she hurried on before he could urge his horse between us.

"Don't mourn him, missy, for you'll see him again," she gabbled quickly and stepped back as the groom thrust between us.

"Let's away, mistress," he said, uneasily. "She's a bad'un and like to cause harm to honest folk."

Behind him the old woman watched me, her eyes bright and shrewd. "He'll return one day," she went on, "but he'll be like a stranger to you and bring danger with him. You'll see him . . . but his sister won't. There's sorrow ahead for you, lady."

"What do you mean? Why should I see him and not his sister? What *do* you mean?"

Her lids fell over her eyes like shutters and her face became closed and expressionless. "You'll see when the time comes," she said and turning her back on me, hunched her shoulders and returned to her former task.

Taking a coin from my purse, I tossed it towards her and was surprised to see a child crawl out of the shadows and retrieve it. For a moment, I had an impression of tangled dark hair and wide pale, almost violet coloured eyes in a thin, sharp face before she bit the coin and hid it away among the ragged garments she wore.

At last I obeyed the urgings of the groom's hand on my reins and allowed him to lead me out of the glade.

"Why are you afraid of her?" I asked when he judged us sufficiently distant and let the horses slow their canter to a walk.

"Some do say she's a witch," he answered.

"And you believe them!" I laughed.

He refused to meet my eyes, but went on stubbornly. "She can do things . . . set spells and such like. Knows things she does, as is going to happen. You stay away from her, mistress, like all sensible folk."

"Wait until you fall in love, John," I said lightly. "I'll wager you'll ask her then for a love potion."

The man shuddered. "Not I — 'tis more like to be poison. Folks say she uses toads and mice and such like in her potions."

I chided him for his foolishness, but was in reality a little uneasy myself. The woman's eyes had been so knowing that I half suspected she could have told me more than she had. Knowing she intended me to think so and visit her again to pay for her prophesies, I was yet curious and found myself wondering what else she would have said if we had been alone and shivered a little as I remembered the 'sorrows' she foretold.

They seemed to begin almost at once; rumours about the Spanish fleet had been rife for months and we treated them as commonplace gossip, but in June Sir Robert rode over, his face grim and his pockets full of little gifts and loving messages for me from Jane.

Retiring to the windowseat with her letter I let the conversation of the men drift over my head while I read her neat writing. As she had thought when last I visited her, she was with child and was obviously filled with happiness at the prospect of becoming a mother. Aunt Campernowne, she reported, had at first tried to keep her old position in the house, treating her as before, but upon finding that Sir Robert had no intention of his wife being treated with anything less than the respect and consideration she deserved, now spent much of her time in her chamber refusing to take an interest in her surroundings — even the prospect of a grandchild seeming of no import to her.

Something Sir Robert said caught my attention and dropping the letter in my lap, I looked up listening to their conversation.

"The country is to be held in a state of readiness," he was saying. "Men are to be ready to light the beacons, which were built on vantage points last year, the moment the fleet is sighted and so taking light from each other give warning in London."

"What has happened?" I asked unable to keep the fear from my voice.

"The Armada has set sail," Conn supplied briefly and at once turned back to the other man. "We are to mobilize I suppose?"

Robert nodded. "According to the directive of last year all able-bodied men are to provide their own weapons and proceed to various strategic parts of the country. You and I, Conn, are to take our band and defend Portsmouth and the coast thereabouts."

"I'll wager the Queen regrets her neglect of the army now. With most of our soldiers in the Low Countries and our inability to bring them home because of the need to keep them between us and the Spaniards in Holland, we are left sadly open to attack. Pray God the seadogs beat the invincible fleet — once they land we shall be defeated by sheer force of numbers. Thank Heaven for 'El Draque' and the fear he strikes into Spanish hearts."

"Raleigh, too," insisted the courtier.

Conn laughed. "Sir Walter as well, then," he agreed. "He has the dash and panache but Drake is the seaman."

Forgetting me, they walked out deep in

arrangements for the morrow, reminding me of nothing so much as two schoolboys planning an escapade. Even when Conn returned alone there was still the light of mischief in his eyes.

"It's not a game, you know," I said, between tears and anger. "Do you really intend to leave us here alone — a house and village filled solely with women and children. What if the Spaniards come?"

"I've heard tell that their manners are most courteous."

"Oh, Conn," I said helplessly. "Don't tease. Y-you might be killed." Despite my attempt at calmness, my voice trembled and my uneven breathing shook my body.

"Would you mind?"

For a moment I stared at him and then I cast myself into his arms, clinging to him with desperate fingers, forgetting my pride, not caring that I had been careful to keep my feelings from him in case he failed to return them.

"Why sweetheart, what's this?" he said gently.

"Conn, I need you here," I sobbed. "Please don't go."

Seeming much pleased at my confession, he covered my wet face in kisses and murmured nonsense until I grew calmer.

"Go, I must," he said, seating himself and taking me on his knee. "Would you have the Inquisition set up in our land?"

I shuddered at the images his words called up and he held me tightly, his cheek resting against my hair. "I'll go, Perditta, but have no fear about my coming back. I've fought the Spaniards before and was a match for them then."

"I did not know."

"It's not an episode I talk about — war is not the adventure the poets would have us believe."

He stared into the distance, his expression bleak and I wondered at the cause.

"I served as a volunteer in the Low Counties and saw enough to make me vow that I would never sit by and see the Spaniards rule England."

At last I understood something behind the reason for his actions with regard to the Jesuit plots and knew that he had handed on information in the hope of foiling any attempt to set a Catholic on the throne and so bring to England religious bigotry and persecution such as Spain knew under the Inquisition.

"I did not know you cared so deeply," I said quietly.

"I have no liking for acting the spy," he replied, "for betraying secrets told to me by men who thought me their fellow."

"Francis Hill hasn't been here since I hid him in the hole," I said, remembering the fugitive priest. "Have the Queen's men taken him?"

"I haven't heard. I daresay the Jesuits are lying low after the fiasco of the Babbington Plot, though I would have thought they would be moving about the country, assessing the reaction to the approaching Spanish fleet."

I shivered at his words, recalled to the dire situation that faced us.

"Must you really go? Surely no-one would miss you."

He held me closer, trying to comfort me with the warmth of his embrace. "What if all counted on not being missed? The Spaniards would find the country open to them should they beat our fleet."

"Think you they will?" I asked fearfully.

The shake he gave his head was decisive. "Our sailors have been practising for years on their treasure ships from the New World — if we can catch them at sea the victory will be ours." He finished on a more sombre note. "If they manage to land there may be a different story; their ships are filled with soldiers, fighting men well equipped and trained and our army has been neglected for years."

Suddenly he put me off his knee and stood up. "If I'm to be away and the times troublesome there's something I had best show you. There's something that even you don't know about."

And taking my arm he led me into the Great Hall, first making sure no-one was about and then opening the cupboard door and taking out the wine and goblets kept there, speaking quickly as he worked.

"Little John Owen is a master of these secrets and never forms a hide, but that he makes a means of escape from it if at all possible." Motioning me closer, Conn climbed inside and I could hear tinder being struck. A candle took flame and

I could see him, bending over the seat set against the far wall. With an effort, he raised the stone slab and revealed a dark gaping hole.

"It's only a short passage," he went on, dropping the slab back in place, "and comes out in the woods beyond the gardens. Little John made use of a stone passage already here — one often finds such things in old buildings that have housed monks. I believe they were sewers such as the Romans used."

I had viewed the thing with horror and now asked nervously if it was accessible from the outside.

Conn laughed at my fears and said that even if the entrance was found, which was unlikely, the stone seat could only be lifted from the inside and showed me the hidden spring which released it.

The rest of the day was spent in a bustle of activity, giving me little time for thought and the next morning he and the able men from the houses nearby were gone, riding off like knights of old, with the sun shining on their hastily burnished weapons. Of late their accoutrements had grown sadly neglected, swords and daggers being put to peaceable use, which blunted their edges and rendered them of little use for warlike purposes. Some had even been unaccountably lost and now their frustrated owners had given up the search and carried anything that came to hand. Pitchforks and scythes and sickles made formidable if unorthodox weapons and the grim purpose on the faces of the men who carried them told plainly that if the need arose they would be used with all the determination shown at Cressy and Agincourt.

Once alone we women returned to our work and the older of the boys left behind hunted out anything suitable left behind by their elders and formed themselves into bands, taking upon themselves the defence of Galliard's Hay and their homes. For a few days they could be seen marching about with old discarded weapons on their shoulders or assiduously attempting to repair broken swords with all the fleeting intense involvement of youth; then the excitement wore off and they were chased back to the fields by their exasperated mothers.

The days grew into weeks and the

hardest part to bear was the lack of news. At last John the groom returned with the news that the men had been stationed on a hill outside Portsmouth which commanded a good view of the town and sea and at first sight of the enemy they were to ride down and defend the harbour at all costs. Only waiting long enough to fill his saddlebags with food from my kitchens and necessities Conn had requested, he rode off again, unwilling to stay longer, lest he should miss an encounter with the Spaniards.

I watched him go and then ordered my horse saddled, glad of an excuse to make the journey to Hawks' Hill. I found Jane as eager as I for news and we discussed the forthcoming possibilities over wine and biscuits, fearful for our menfolk, but caught up in the air of excited optimism that covered the country now that at last we were to come to grips with the enemy that had plagued us for so long.

"If we win it will be an end to fearing the Spanish," said Jane.

"We'll win," I said, more confidently than I felt. "Conn says we will and you know that he can never be wrong." I looked over my shoulder and leaned forward to ask cautiously "My Aunt — how is she taking this?"

"I think she's praying for a Spanish victory," Jane confided and then looked worried by her unthinking confession. "She spends her days in her room, on her knees, telling her beads. I scarcely see her for which I must confess I'm grateful."

"Oh, Jane!" I cried impulsively. "I'm sorry, how I wish it could be pleasanter for you."

"I've Robert and the coming babe. I learned not to expect love or affection from my parents when I was quite a small child . . . Dudley I *do* miss . . . "

She blinked a tear from her lashes and took up the embroidery that had lain forgotten in her lap.

"Have you heard tell of an old woman called Grannie Green?" I asked, suddenly recalling the shelter in the woods near Galliard's Hay and the prophecy of its inhabitant. Quickly I told my cousin of the old woman's forecast that Dudley would return, neglecting only to mention that she would not see him herself.

"How wonderful it would be," she said, her eyes shining. "Do you believe her? Does she seem to know the future or is she a charlatan?"

I shrugged a little. "Who can tell? The groom thought her a witch and a fraud."

"A witch!" Jane was horrified, the colour abruptly leaving her face. "Oh, Perditta, if she's a witch you must have nothing to do with her. She could be dangerous . . . such women are evil."

"I'm not sure she is one," I told her thoughtfully. "More like a poor lonely old woman who ekes out a living by playing on the fears and hopes of others. She had a child there . . . with the most beautiful eyes I've ever seen. Almost violet and enormous."

Jane shuddered and hastily crossed herself. "She must be one, too," she said, her voice shaking.

"She's only a child — about ten I should guess," I laughed.

"Children can be in the power of Satan — age makes no difference. Promise me you'll not go there again. You should take a priest and some men and turn them off your land."

I was amused and a little disturbed to find my gentle Jane so fierce and unfeeling. "There are no men, even if I wished to remove them," I pointed out.

"As soon as Conn comes home," she urged and I murmured noncomittally, soothing her fears and agreeing to nothing, turning the conversation to her forthcoming babe in the expectation that she would forget the disturbing topic of the old woman.

However, as I rode home, I found my horse turning, almost without rotation, in the direction of the sheltered glade. As before smoke drifted up from the open fire, Grannie Green appearing in the low doorway of the hut as I approached, her expression without surprise and I knew the uneasy thought that she appeared almost to have expected my arrival.

"He'll be back," she said as I drew rein.

"Who?"

"The one you worry over — and without ever riding down from the hill."

I was startled by her mention of the hill, for as far as I could see there was no possibility of her having come upon that knowledge.

There was a movement behind her and I smiled at the child clutching her skirt and peering at me with wide, pale eyes.

"What's your name, poppet?" I asked.

The old woman glanced down. "Linnet, so it please your lady," she supplied and looked from me to the girl, her eyes suddenly narrowed. Roughly she pushed the girl forward. "There's your lady — make your curtsey to her."

Violet eyes met mine as I puzzled over the old woman's words, but as I returned the child's gaze I had the strangest feeling of affinity, for all the difference in age I knew there could be friendship between us.

"That's right, lady," said the other woman, seeming to read my thoughts. "There's ties between you — more than the bonds of service or kinship. Some folks are bound together and you and my Linnet are two such. First you'll do her a kindness and then she'll serve you and yours for the rest of her life — and not even be able to rest then."

I felt she had gone far enough and

interrupted to ask bluntly if she wanted me to take the girl into my household.

To my surprise, for I thought that had been her aim, she shook her head and drew the child against her with a possessive gesture.

"Not yet," she answered fiercely. "You'll have her longer than I will. She's mine now and will bide with me for a while yet."

"As you will," I made answer, growing tired of the conversation and thinking of my two babes waiting for me in their nursery at Galliard's Hay, but she stopped me as I nudged my horse with my heels.

"You'll be another Sarah," she said suddenly, "but your boy will be the death of you."

Hesitating only momentarily, I flicked the reins and trotted across the glade, wondering at her words. The only Sarah I knew was in the Bible and had a son when she was thought to be past the age for child bearing . . . was *that* what she meant? I was to think much upon her words, but at the moment discarded them, content to hug the knowledge to myself that I was almost certainly with child again and that *this* time it must be a son I carried.

My hopes were not to be fulfilled for even before the possibility became a certainty the hope was gone and such old news by the time Conn returned that I kept my disappointment to myself and did not even mention it to him. Indeed so full were they of their adventures that I would have been hard put to wedge a word in between theirs.

"So many rumours and impossible tales flew from around that it was hard to tell true from false," said Conn. "However it is sure that the invasion threat is over and the Armada scattered."

We were in the Great Hall, crowded together to hear his story, even the grooms and outside servants having joined us. Conn stood halfway up the stairs and addressed us all, while we hung upon his words like the audience at a theatre.

"As you know we were posted to Portsmouth to guard the town and harbour from enemy attack. We had a clear view of the sea, but never a sight of the enemy — we came home without ever riding down from the hill."

The very words the old woman had used gave me pause and I glanced round surreptitiously hoping no-one had noticed the start I had given. All attention was on Conn and I turned back to him, observing with pride his air of command and thinking how handsome he appeared, his skin tanned from exposure to the elements and his soldierly bearing accentuated by his recent command.

"The Spanish fleet was sighted off the Lizard on the 19th of July," he was saying, his listeners hanging upon his words. "Howard brought our fleet out of Plymouth and with Drake, Hawkins, Frobisher and others, kept up a running fight for a week. Our losses were practically nil, the Spanish shot going over our smaller ships, with us firing into the enemies sides. Our seamen out maneuvered the Spanish galleons and when they took refuge in Calais Howard sent fireships in among them and they upped anchor and fled — straight into the teeth of a gale, which by God's providence was awaiting them in the channel! They ran before it and being unmaneuverable by their size and design were dispersed and wrecked upon the rocky coasts of Cornwall and Ireland. Some it's even said were driven ashore as far away as Scotland."

Lusty cheers greeted his story, men clapping each other on the shoulder or kissing their neighbour if she happened to be female. Above the din Conn shouted for a barrel of ale to be broached and soon everyone held a brimming tankard.

"A toast," cried Conn. "To England and Elizabeth!"

We all shouted heartily and downed our ale in a fervour of loyalty and relief at our deliverance from the foe who had plagued us for so long.

"Do you really think it's the end?" I asked later when we were alone.

"For a while, at least. Philip of Spain counted on the English Catholics rising to join him when they heard of his invasion plans. He had not thought that they would care more for Queen and country than religion when the time came for them to decide. I doubt not that the fanatics will try again . . . in a few years the Jesuits will return with new plans and plots, but for the moment we may rest easy."

After the excitements of the last few weeks the rest of the summer passed quietly with nothing to disturb our peace and content save the news from Hawks' Hill that my Aunt Campernowne, not caring for the outcome of the Armada, had taken herself off to a convent in France. Apart from sparing a thought for the novices who would soon be feeling the effect of her tongue, the information had little impact for me, but I knew that Jane would be easier without the presence of her mother.

In late October I journeyed over to Hawks' Hill to await the arrival of my cousin's baby, taking with me the village woman who had assisted at the births of my children. Her pains began a few days later and we had hopes of an easy outcome; however when she had been in labour for several hours with little progress we knew that she needed more help than either of us could give.

Facing the village woman across the bed I desperately asked for her advice. "There must be *something* we can do."

"There's only old Grannie Green," she said reluctantly. "I've heard tell she can help sometimes."

Under my directions Robert rode off, glad, poor man, of something to do, and quickly returned with the old woman. She entered the room quietly, not at all overcome by her surroundings and stood looking down at Jane's writhing form.

"Tis a breach", she announced "and she's small."

"We know," I told her impatiently. "Can you do anything?"

"I can try," she answered and I suddenly knew renewed hope at her calm words.

Taking a packet of herbs from her pocket, she quickly brewed a noxious drink and forced it between Jane's pallid lips. Waiting until the restorative had taken effect, she motioned the village woman and me away and bent over the striving woman on the bed.

At Jane's cry the village midwife started forward, but knowing that this was my cousin's only chance, I held her back, listening to Grannie Green's voice as she cajolled and encouraged, her calm tones full of firm purpose. As the minutes passed I felt the perspiration break out, clenching my fists with tension and anxiety.

A low moan came from behind the bed curtains followed by a long silence during which I held my breath with dread. Suddenly the most welcome sound in the world echoed about the room and I turned weak with relief, unable to move even when the old woman appeared with a babe in her arms and it was the midwife who started forward to take it from her, while the other turned back to attend to her patient.

"She must never have any more — it'ud be the death of her," Grannie Green said, when her work was done and she was relaxing by the fire for a few minutes before starting back to her hovel. "Mind you tell her."

I promised and looking at Jane's sleeping figure and grey, fatigued face, realized how near death she had been, but for the moment my prevailing emotion was relief and a certain euphoria that it was all over.

Some days later, when she had recovered

somewhat and was able to admire her sleeping son, I told her what the old woman had said.

She smiled at the red, crumpled face of her baby, and seemed uninterested in my warning.

"I must be grateful for her help," she answered, "but I could wish that she had not been sent for. It worries me that she has been into my house — perhaps even given a hold over my son."

"She seems wise in such matters, and we had done all we could."

Jane stroked the baby's pink fist. "Who's to say that the baby would not have been born without her aid?"

I understood then; my cousin preferred not to accept her advice and so would reject all possibility that the old woman was right.

Jane suddenly raised her head and looked fully at me. "I'll thank you, Perditta, not to mention such foolishness to Robert," she said, her voice unusually firm. "I refuse to believe in the sayings of an illiterate, uneducated old woman."

She turned back to her baby and I knew that as far as she was concerned the matter was closed. Conn said it was none of my business, but the episode made me uneasy until the months passed and Jane regained her strength and vitality, seeming stronger and more happy than ever before. Watching her glowing countenance I decided the witch-woman had been mistaken and felt able to relax once more.

11

BUSY with our own affairs, we had been a little out of touch with the world, but by November news of Robert Dudley, Earl of Leicester's death had filtered through to our rural part of Hampshire. He had long been the Queen's favourite and many were the rumours spread abroad about them, and naturally the same suspicion had entered Conn's and my head since we had given serious thought to my parentage. Across the room, we exchanged glances, but neither then nor ever after did we speak about it; by mutual consent it was a forbidden subject.

Sir Robert, who had brought the news was unaware of our reaction and went on to tell us that Leicester had already been ailing when he took command of the army at Tilbury in July.

"It's the end of an era," he said. "The Queen's men grow old in her service and there are few to take their place.

Burghley has trained his son Robert to take his place, but he's only the son not the father."

We all agreed knowledgably and for a while we allowed ourselves the luxury of complaint, until growing tired of setting the world to rights, I asked after the welfare of his baby.

"Have you decided upon a name? Poppet is all very well at a few weeks — but he can hardly carry such a title through life!"

"Thomas, doubtless to be termed Tom," smiled Robert. "You and Conn will come and do your duty as Godparents at his Christening?"

"Of course," we agreed readily, but I at least had to suppress a pang of envy at thought of the lusty boy in the cradle at Hawks' Hill.

My own two girls were growing apace. Beth at over two was a lively toddler, while Kate hovered on the verge of walking and showed every sign of the temper that her red-haired sister should have owned. Beth was a sunny child and altogether more placid and content that the mercurial Kate. I loved them dearly but had a longing for a dark-haired lad, who would be the image of his father to tease and charm me by turns.

Christmas seemed to arrive early that year, creeping up quietly and then springing on me while I was still busy with other things. Galliard's Hay was filled with guests and their retainers, the Summers as well as Jane and Robert spending the holiday with us. Freed from worry over the Spanish invasion and filled with euphoria at our victory, we were all happier than we had been for years and the old house seemed to echo our feelings and encompass us in a cocoon of warmth and security. Never had we spent such a festive season, joy seemed to be ours as we gave expression to the relief we felt after years of suppressed fears.

Afterwards I was to be glad that we had had that Christmas, but at the time there was no intimation of pending tragedy and we were happy to enjoy ourselves with our kin and friends.

No sooner was Christmas over than winter descended upon us with a freezing grip. Too cold to snow, the countryside was icebound, the ground hard with deep frost and all water, save the deepest well, frozen iron hard. Birds fell dead with cold from the branches of trees and starving foxes ventured into the stables in search of food.

I took a basket to Grannie Green and found her and the child thin and apathetic as they struggled to keep warm in their freezing hovel. The local folk soon ran through their meagre stores and applied to me for help. Eventually even the cellars of Galliard's Hay were sadly depleted and I viewed the long months until they could be replenished with some apprehension. Before the thaw came our salt barrels were almost empty and the dovecot lacking most of its inhabitants.

Snow fell at last and for once even the adults greeted its arrival with pleasure. The temperature rose with the first white flake and with the lifting of the dreadful cold that froze the blood of man and beast. Travel was again possible and the journey to Alton could be made to refill empty larders and cellars.

After that nature seemed to relent and as though to make up for her cruelty, spring came early and was doubly beautiful for our winter ordeal. This made it even harder to bear when the local cattle fell ill, aborting the calves we all hoped for to replace the stock we had killed for meat.

Despite the weather and nodding spring flowers, people went about the nearby houses and fields with long faces, their mood ugly as they looked for a reason for their misfortune. Soon the dreaded word 'witch' was heard and before long everyone was convinced that they had been 'overlooked' and their cows spellbound by someone with the evil eye. Their choice fell, as it was obvious it would, on Grannie Green and matters came to a head one day when yet another cow lost its calf and the villagers lost their tempers and all sense of humanity and common sense.

I had been riding in the woods when alerted by distant shouts and cries. I spurred towards the sounds and came upon a crowd of men and women from the houses near Galliard's Hay, surrounding a wide pond among the trees. Their interest was centred on something in the water and they had no idea of my approach until I was among them.

Staring over their heads I saw that what I had taken for a bundle of rags floating on the surface of the pond was in fact the bound figure of a woman. Something tugged at my skirt and I looked down into huge, tormented violet eyes. Beyond speech the child could only point towards her grandmother and utter unintelligible cries.

Suddenly beside myself with rage and horror at their action, I set my mare to plunging and cavorting while I laid about me with my riding whip. Surprised by my presence and demoralized by my anger the villagers drew back and quickly dispersed, slinking away like guilty children.

At last we were alone, even John, my groom, had gone and I knew that if we were to save the old woman we would have to act quickly. Urging my horse into the water, I leaned out of the saddle to catch hold of her trailing, sodden clothing and pulled her ashore. Immediately the girl flung herself upon the soaking bundle, clinging to the inert woman and wailing her grief and fright aloud.

Putting her aside I felt for a heartbeat and reaching into my pocket for a knife, cut the bonds that tied the woman's thumbs and toes together.

One look at her livid face was enough to dispel all hope, but nevertheless I rolled her on to her back and leaned hard on her ribs to force out the water that filled her lungs. She remained flaccid and horribly limp under my hands, and giving up the useless attempt I took the weeping girl into my arms and was trying to comfort her when Conn galloped up and flung himself from the saddle.

"They tried her by water," I told him bitterly. "They needed a scapegoat for their lost calves and chose this old woman. They *disgust* me!"

"They believe her a witch," said Conn. "Not everyone has your disbelief in such things. Is she dead?"

I nodded and said the girl must come with us. Conn frowned, seeming to dislike the idea, but only hesitated momentarily before putting a hand on her thin shoulder. At his touch the decision was taken from us, for she started to her feet with a shriek of fear and ran, fleet as a hare, for the surrounding trees.

"Well, that's that," said Conn with a certain amount of satisfaction in his voice and I knew that he was glad to be relieved of the moral duty to look after the girl.

"Poor child," I said, looking after her. "How will she live?"

"She'll make her way to the nearest town and become either a thief or a beggar," he said casually, but I could not dismiss her so easily and often wondered what had become of her.

Before we left the clearing Conn ducked his head and went into the hut to emerge a few seconds later with a small, grey bundle under one arm.

"There's nothing of interest there — save this," he reported.

"It's her cat — I've often seen it here."

"What shall I do with it? Shall she join her mistress?" He indicated the calm surface of the pond. "If she's her familiar it would be best."

"Oh, Conn," I cried in exasperation,

not sure if he was teasing or really believed the old woman was a witch. "Surely you don't — "

"No," he answered evenly, "but the villagers do. You've already shown you are on the woman's side. If you take what they believe is her familiar, they may well turn their fear and hate to you."

I laughed in disbelief and shook my head.

"They are ignorant, superstitious peasants. Let one child throw a fit as you pass by and they'll accuse you of putting the evil eye on it."

"After I fed them through the winter — no, they are more grateful than that," I assured him. "Let me take the cat. She'll keep the mice down in the house. The villagers were too frightened to come here so you need have no fear that any will recognize the animal."

I held out my hands and reluctantly Conn dropped the cat into my arms. As pale as smoke her fur was velvet smooth and soft as silk. Bright yellow eyes looked into mine as I soothed her and as though reassured, she began to purr and allowed me to carry her home.

Of course I had been mistaken when I declared none would know her. Despite their fear it became apparent that practically everyone in the house and locality had paid a surreptitious visit to Grannie Green at some time or other in search of medicine, which she brewed from wild herbs or more noxious substances about which she was equally knowledgeable. To make matters worse the cat transferred her allegiance to me and followed me about like a silent shadow.

Her worth as a mouse catcher was undeniable but I often caught Conn eyeing her with an unfathomable expression which filled me with unease, for I had become fond of her, while she treated Conn with wary disdain and indifference.

"I vow that cat should have been called Greymalkin," he exploded one day, when she had removed herself ostentatiously as soon as he entered the room where we were sitting. "If I were a superstitious man I'd swear she was a soul bewitched!"

"Why do you think I named her nothing more exciting than Tibs?" I asked coolly. "A cat answering to the name of Tibs could hardly be accused of being anything other than a normal, ordinary household catcher of mice."

Both Jane and I were pregnant that summer; our babies due within a day or so of each other, we grew in size together and made baby clothes and plans for our offspring as women will. Remembering Grannie Green's warning I watched my cousin carefully, but even to my anxious eyes childbearing agreed with her and she acquired a new bloom and poise as her girth increased. When I mentioned tentatively that Robert should be made aware of the possible danger, she recalled to me my word not to tell him in sharper tones than she had ever used to me and the best I could do was to prevail upon her to allow the physician from Alton to attend her should the need arise. With that promise I had to be content and, trying to hide my apprehension, went about the business of stocking the capacious larders of Galliard's Hay with the produce of our fields and garden.

The golden months passed uneventfully and I thought the ugly matter of witchcraft had been forgotten until the very thing Conn had forseen happened; a child in one of the nearby houses threw a fit, and at once the inhabitants recalled all their suspicions and were to be seen again, huddled together in whispering groups. Their ill-humour appeared to go no further than gossiping and I was determined to ignore their suspicions and continue as usual, visiting the village with advice and food for those who needed them, until one day I became aware that Tibs, who had accompanied me as was her habit, had vanished. Looking about the dusty track between the houses, I could see no sign of her and turned back into the house I had just left to ask if she was there. Something in their manner as they disavowed all knowledge of her, made me suspicious and I hurried outside again in time to see a group of half-grown youths slip round the side of a house, their manner both furtive and excited.

Convinced that they were up to mischief, I hurried after them and rounded the corner in time to see them cross a field and slip in among the surrounding trees.

Impeded by my condition I bunched up my skirts and made what speed I could after them. The fact that I was sure that one of them had been carrying a struggling, grey bundle made me determined to catch them.

Intent upon their business they were unaware that I had followed them and I came up on them as they climbed the steep side of a wooded slope. Taking refuge behind a tree, I watched to see what they were about, but when a rope was thrown over a branch and the end tied to the squirming animal they held, I shouted and dashed from my hiding place, running up the hill towards the boys.

They started guiltily at my cry and Tibs seized the opportunity to scratch her way free, a grey streak that vanished among the trees with terrified speed.

Wild with rage, I spluttered furious threats and would willingly have beaten them with my own hands, but as I scrambled upwards my foot caught in a bare, gnarled root and my ankle twisted under me. Losing balance I fell backwards and the white, frightened faces of the youths, staring wide-eyed, not at me but at something above and beyond me, was the last thing I remembered as I plunged into darkness.

I have no idea how long I was unconscious, but I think only a few moments, for when I opened my eyes I was still alone, but knew from the sounds that someone was descending toward me. A figure dressed in white robes appeared and bent solicitously over me, its glinting halo hanging unheeded over one ear, while behind its thin shoulders rose a magnificent, slightly battered pair of pink wings.

I closed my eyes against such a vision and swallowed weakly. "Are you an Angel?" I asked.

"I'm Linnet, lady," the being replied in practical tones and I sighed with relief, laughing weakly until pain stabbed me.

"Run for help," I cried, clutching my stomach as though I would hold the babe in place. "Oh, quickly. Quickly!"

But even then I knew it was too late, even as I had known all along that the child I carried was the longed for boy.

Conn and men from the house came running with a hurdle lifted from a fence to carry me home. Mary, my maid, and the midwife from the village did all they could, but by evening all hope was gone and my puny, too small son was wrapped in his swaddling bands that were also his shroud, and laid to rest before he had ever lived.

Jane hurried to my side and Conn stayed by me day and night, hiding his own grief to comfort me, but I was lost in the depths of despair, caring nothing save for my own sorrow. One day I awoke to find a violet eyed child standing beside the bed, clutching a cat in her arms.

"So you got home," I murmured to Tibs, finding a slight pleasure in her presence. "And you, Linnet?"

"The Master says I'm to stay," she said.

"Do you want to?" She nodded, and I remembered something. "How did you come to be dressed as an angel?" I asked, interested in spite of myself.

"I took up with some players. We was doing a Mystery play at Alton and I was an angel, but the man hit me and I ran away . . . and came here to find you."

Losing interest at such a mundane explanation, I turned away and closed my eyes, taking small comfort from the warm body of Tibs pressed against me as she slept on the brocade bedcover.

Almost against my will, my body regained its strength but my mind remained dull and oppressed. Nothing aroused me from the depths of my despair. Conn sent to London for a harpsichord, such as the Queen herself played upon, knowing I had learned as a child and had often wished for one, but even that failed to hold my interest for more than a few moments. I spent most of my time sitting in the window of my bedchamber, staring out at the gardens with unseeing eyes, mourning my son and awaiting the death Grannie Green had promised. Sunk in my own sorrow I had no thought to spare for others and it never occurred to me that my husband could be suffering as much as I.

Let the world go on without me, I thought bitterly. I have had enough of it and turned my back on all their blandishments . . . until one day a few weeks after my accident I heard voices from the Great Hall. At first I took no notice, apart from noting that someone had left my door open allowing the voices to disturb me. Then, in spite of myself, I became interested. Something in the rough tones that carried to my ear spoke of desperation and fear. The man who spoke most often, like an actor taking the leading part, while the others mumbled a chorus, seemed to be pleading, begging almost.

I recognized Conn giving a short, decisive negative reply and filled with curiosity crept to the door hoping to learn the cause of the disturbance, but although the voices were louder, I still could not make out what they were saying and for the first time since I lost the baby, I left my room and ventured out on to the landing to lean over the bannister.

Conn was facing a group of men from the village with an air of grim determination. They appeared to be in abject misery, hanging their heads and with bowed shoulders, while their spokesman seemed to be pleading a cause they already knew was lost.

"It was the young 'uns," said their spokesman. "We didn't know about it — and even then 'twas only the cat. They didn't intend any harm to your lady."

"You must all go," Conn said immoveably. "I want the village cleared by Sunday."

"But — we've nowhere to go, Sir Conn! Have pity on our wives and children."

"You had none on mine. My wife carried my heir."

The man could only murmur their sorrow, shifting uncomfortably from one foot to the other, twisting their caps in their hands.

"We'll send the lads involved to you," offered the man desperately. "Do what you like with them — beat them, send them away, anything you like."

"Sunday," repeated Conn, his face implaccable.

At his resolute tones a collective moan seemed to escape the men; these were respectable workers, but with the loss of their homes and livelihood they and their families faced destitution. Some even fell to their knees, while others covered their faces to hide their emotions. Conn made a dismissive gesture and turned away, but I could stand no more and ran to the head of the stairs.

"Conn," I call commandingly and at my voice all eyes turned upon me. "Conn," I went on, sweeping down to stop a few steps away from the floor. "You cannot mean this."

My husband came forward to meet me, leaning on the newelpost with one arm as he looked up. "I do indeed. And you, of all people, should want the instigators of your sorrow punished."

"What good would it do?"

"Why none, my dear, but even the Bible speaks of an eye for an eye."

"Do two wrongs make matters right? It would be wrong to turn those people away. They have done nothing — "

"Save gossip and spread rumours and lies," Conn put in viciously, "until their children were so inflamed by their elders' suspicions that they took action upon themselves."

"They have done nothing," I went on,

"except talk and speculate, which is a human failing. Even the boys intended me no harm and as proof of that they ran for help."

"Because they were afraid of the effect of their actions."

"Doubtless — but surely that makes their action in coming to you even better. I could not have recognized them." Conn hesitated and I pressed home my advantage. "Forget the matter this once . . . and I am sure there will be an end to all this bother and superstitious fears." I turned to the village men, now regarding me hopefully. "I am certain that witchcraft will be mentioned no more and that no-one regards my cat as anything other than a normal animal."

They murmured an eager assent, pressing forward to assure me that none of them would give such nonsense a thought in the future and we all turned expectantly to the master of Galliard's Hay.

"Very well," he said, at last, having considered the matter. "I'll forget your behaviour this once, but I shall not be so lenient another time."

Their relief was almost pitiful and I thanked Heaven that the man who held such sway over them was as merciful as Conn. As they turned to go, he stopped them.

"Remember, you have your mistress to thank for my mercy," he said.

Pulling their forelocks, they bowed humbly, outdoing each other with their loud thanks. Expressing lifelong gratitude and service, they backed to the door and thankfully left our presence.

"I hope they've learned their lesson," commented my husband, something in his voice making my eyes fly to his face.

"Would you really have turned them out?"

"Of course," he answered calmly.

Something in his attitude had been puzzling me. Usually my husband was not a vengeful man; his violent rages required action at once, not some weeks later. It was totally unlike him to wait so long to deal with the culprits and usually just, it was even less like him to take vengeance on the innocent families of the offenders. Recalling the open door and the overloud voices I caught my breath with sudden suspicion.

"You arranged it!" I accused.

He kissed me for answer. "I had to do something to arouse you from your apathy," he said. "And I knew that you liked nothing better than righting a wrong. I must confess I counted on your acute sense of justice to bring you out of your room — not to mention your curiosity."

"Oh, Conn," I cried, holding him close. "What a selfish woman I am. I thought of no-one but myself. You must have suffered as much as I."

"Doubtless we'll have our boy in time — and now there's Beth and Kate to be grateful for," he answered stoically and I wondered anew at the man I had married, for I knew beyond all doubt how much he wanted an heir.

Jane continued in health and I truly felt that my worries over the forthcoming event were merely foolishness. She began her labour late one evening and by the time I arrived the next morning, had already lost her bloom. Dark rings encircled her sunken eyes and she seemed pitifully weak and thin.

"It's all that raspberry leaf tisane I drank," she tried to joke, seeing the anxiety I was unable to hide.

Leaving her for a moment, I discovered that the physician from Alton had already been sent for and hurried back to her side. All I could do was to sponge her forehead with vinegar and hold her hand while a dreadful fear grew in me.

The doctor came but after a brief examination admitted he could do little, offering to save the child at the expense of the mother. This Robert angrily refused and we were left to fall back on the old remedies, used by ages of women before us. At last, when we thought all hope was gone, the baby was born. Giving it scarcely a glance, I focused all my attention on Jane, lying flat and quiet, hardly seeming to breath, so much had that final effort taken from her. Wearily she roused her heavy eyelids and thinking to reassure her, I said the child was healthy, but this was not what she had on her mind and with a great effort, she whispered,

"My babes . . . *you'll* care for them."

"You'll look after them yourself, never fear," I tried to comfort her, but she gave the merest shake of her head, staring up at me entreatingly.

"You know I will care for them as if they were my own," I said, my voice husky with unshed tears, "but you'll tend them yourself — "

She sighed on a long drawn out breath and I turned away as Robert hurried to take my place at the bedside.

Jane died as dusk fell that evening, slipping away as imperceptibly as the winter's day. We tried to comfort ourselves that she had left a baby behind, but in my heart I would have readily given the child to have back my cousin. Robert was quiet and withdrawn, only his tensed shoulders and tight mouth betraying his emotions.

"I know childbirth is dangerous," he said later, sitting in his chair and toying with the food we had persuaded him to take, "but she appeared so well . . . so full of health and energy."

I looked at his bowed head and decided not to mention the old woman's prophecy; no good would come of it and I might very well add to his grief. Reaching out blindly, he took my hand and held it in a grip so tight that I thought the bones might crack. Offering the only comfort I could, I drew him to me and cradled his head against my bosom rocking him like a baby as I murmured endearments.

He accepted my gesture with relief, speaking with his voice muffled by my arms. "You, of all people must know that Jane was not my only love . . . but she was such a good, simple woman, so kind and thoughtful that I grew to love her as she deserved. We were content — "

A sound and movement in the doorway made me look up to see Conn standing in the shadowy entrance. How long he had been there, there was no way of telling, but something in his attitude made me loosen my hold of Robert, who sat up and stretched a hand to Conn.

My husband came forward at once to take the offered hand in a warm grasp. "I came as soon as I heard," he said and looked at me, his glance questioning above the bowed, fair head.

The tears I had been controlling all

day, slithered down my cheeks and he stretched out his free hand to gather me close in a comforting embrace. Suddenly I realized how glad I was of his firm, strong presence and I gratefully gave up my role of comforter which I had played all day and allowed myself to be consoled in turn.

In the first wave of his grief, Robert sought relief from his sorrow by returning to the Court and taking up his old life of Queen's man. Hawks' Hill was given over to the care of servants and I took the two children to live with us at Galliard's Hay . . . and so it was that our nursery held members of the male sex after all, but in a manner which no-one could have foreseen.

12

IT was not many months before I realized that all was not well with Jane's new baby. At first I tried to convince myself that he was a late developer, but when his second Christmas came and Will, as he had been christened, still showed no signs of recognition or interest, I knew that there was more than a little wrong with him.

So big at birth that he had cost his mother's life, he had continued to thrive physically and now was a beautiful blond child, the pride of any nursery, save that he lay in his cradle, blank of face and content, gazing at the ceiling with empty blue eyes. He was the darling of his nurse, who declared she had never known such a good baby, but his placid indifference filled me with disquiet and I often crept into the nursery to shake his rattle or show him a pretty, new toy in the hope that he would reach out one of his chubby hands for it.

"We'd best tell Robert," said a voice heavily behind me and I turned to find Conn at my elbow.

For a moment I stared up at him in open surprise. "I did not know you suspected," I said at last.

"I've thought he wasn't so quick as our girls were," he said, as we leaned over the cradle, its occupant placidly ignoring our existence, "but I've noticed how you have watched him and how often you have tried to attract his attention." He sighed heavily. "I'll tell Robert in my next letter."

"Not yet," I cried quickly. "Give him a little longer. He may improve — and it would be such a blow for Robert to bear."

"It's time he came and saw his children. It's over a year since Jane died and in all that time he's not been home to attend to his affairs or to see after his children."

"I write regularly. I believe he is trying to hide his sorrow in work."

Conn snorted. "At Court! More like he's returned to his old life without thought to his country estates. The boys are his responsibility."

"I promised Jane that I would care for them."

"Of course. And I know that it comforted you somewhat in your loss, but they have a father and should grow up knowing him." He patted my hand. "We'll give the boy until spring and if he's made no progress by then, his father must be made aware of the fact."

I had to agree with him, but my heart ached for the child and I prayed for some miracle that would unlock the tiny closed mind. Robert sent gifts and excuses but failed to come himself. I think that Conn's disclosure kept him away rather than brought him to Galliard's Hay and since then I have noticed that some people have this horror of the feeble-minded, choosing to ignore their presence rather than accept them as they are.

By the time Will was four he had attained the achievements of a babe of six months or so and with the support of a cushion could sit up and occasionally reach towards something that had taken his fancy. Beth was ever careful and gentle with him, seeming to accept his limitations with equanimity, but Kate was impatient with his slowness, her own mercurial mind always seeking new interests with the speed and dash of a butterfly. Tom ignored his brother; busy with boyish pursuits, he had no time or interest in babies or other children less able than he and I must admit that I viewed my nephew Tom with mixed feelings. At five he was he was plainly a mirror image of my Uncle Campernowne, with nothing of the gentle Jane in him. He was big for his age and bullied when he could. Kate and he were like vinegar and oil, the very antipathy of each other and fought upon all occasions. Somewhat to my amazement, Beth followed him about like a shadow, his faithful follower in all his doings. Sunny and placid herself she viewed his determined character with admiration, taking part in all his schemes and escapades with enthusiasm, even when she was left to take the blame upon herself, for Tom soon proved himself adept at escaping unscathed from the adventures he inaugurated.

Late in the spring of 1596, Sir Robert made known by letter that he had married again, a widow with three children of her own and some years older than himself.

"A fortuitous choice," Conn remarked dryly, tossing the sheet of heavy paper on to the table. "As the lady is related to the Cecils, Robert can claim kinship with Lord Burghley."

"It must be a lovematch," I declared. "I am glad for him. He says he intends to open up Hawks' Hill and live there — at least during the summer."

"Doubtless he'll want the boys to live with him, though they scarcely know him."

I furrowed my brow in thought. During the seven years which had lapsed since my cousin's death, Robert Varley had at first visited us not at all, but of late he had made a yearly call, treating his older son to all manner of delights, so that the boy looked upon him as the provider of largess. But of his younger son he took little notice, beyond that which duty dictated. I was quite aware of the distaste kept hidden at the back of his blue eyes as he glanced down at the simple child, who even now showed no signs of walking, instead rolling himself everywhere in the little cart we had had made for him.

"He'll want Tom," I agreed, "but what of Will? He has no sympathy for him."

Conn shrugged. "Perhaps he blames him for his mother's death. I've heard that it can be so."

Shaking my head, I sighed and picked up the linen cap I was embroidering. "No — it's his condition, it disgusts him. He only sees the trembling, useless limbs and dribbling mouth. He never notices his smile or the love in his eyes, which he can't express. *You* give him affection and understanding, why can't his own father?"

"Because he never stays long enough to see beyond the idiot that confronts him. Pity him for Jane's death, don't condemn him because he could not stay to face life without her."

"Do you really think he cared that much for her? That her death made such a difference?"

"Don't you?"

I raised my eyes fleetingly to my husband's steady gaze and looked away quickly unable to meet his eyes. "I — don't know."

"Well, it's over and done with now." He paused reflectively. "Though it will be interesting to see the new Lady Varley. I wonder what sort of wife she will make him."

I wondered too and during the next few days found myself often pausing in my work to contemplate the matter. I had told Tom of his new step-mother and was a little surprised to find how easily he took the situation, only asking with an avaricious glint in his eye, if he would live with his father now.

"I expect so," I told him, "but we must wait and see. Many gentlemen's sons live away from home . . . to further their education or to learn about other households and etiquette."

"What about Will?" he demanded. "They'll not want him, no-one would."

Sighing I recalled the many times I had tried to instill some sense of brotherly love between them, but from the very first, Tom had made no attempt to hide his contempt for his brother.

"He has as much right as you to your

father's protection," I told him sternly.

"My father doesn't regard him at all. He wishes he had died."

Under its own volition my hand reached out and dealt him a smart box on the ear. "Never let me hear you say that again."

"It's true — it's true," he sobbed, holding his ear, his face red with fury. With a distinct look of my uncle, he stamped his foot and ran from the room.

Very often as we waited the arrival of the newlyweds I prayed that the new Lady Varley would be an understanding, motherly person who would take poor Will to her sympathetic bosom and cherish him as I did, but one look when at last they did arrive, shattered my foolish dreams.

Lady Varley was tall and slim and elegant from the tip of her wired lace collar, that rose fan-like behind her head, to the toes of her satin shoes that peeped from under her enormously wide farthingale. Her pale, autocratic face, under the velvet hat she wore was calm and expressionless, as her shrewd eyes examined me.

Dropping into a curtsey, I wished that I had not spent the morning in the kitchen garden helping the maids to pick raspberries and hid my stained hands among the folds of my skirt, but a twitch of her thin nose told me that she had not missed my gesture and I lifted my chin as I invited her into the house.

I knew that if I was to save Will from this cold woman, I must appeal at once to his father and hope that Sir Robert still had the sensibility and kindness I had once known. Consequently, I went in search of him as soon as I was able and found him in the garden, enjoying the last warmth of the sun. Looking up at my approach, he smiled and held out his hand.

"Join me here, Perditta," he said, drawing me down to sit beside him on the stone seat. "At times like this I wonder why I stay in smoky, busy London when I could enjoy the peace of the countryside."

"Why do you, then?" I asked.

He lifted his shoulders eloquently. "If I stayed here I would doubtless soon be pining for town and the Court."

"I've been talking to your wife," I said, not willing to lead up to the subject. "About the boys."

He opened his eyes and dazzled by the sun squinted at me. "Aha," he said. "I knew you would not be eager to part with them, but we can no longer take advantage of your goodness."

"It's not that," I told him impatiently. "I've enjoyed having them. In some way they've made up for the lack of boys in our own nursery." I paused knowing I must be careful and speak diplomatically. "Lady Varley says you want both the boys to live with you."

He nodded, his eyes watchful and I knew that he was uncomfortable about his wife's plans for his younger son.

"Do you think it's fair to her?" I hurried on. "To put such a change upon her, a newlywed and not yet settled into her new home? Of course she will do her duty, as she sees it, but to ask her to shoulder the burden of Will, seems a little hard. She seems a delicate, high-minded woman and I own to a little surprise that you should treat her so."

Waiting for his reply, I stole a glance at him and found him watching me thoughtfully, a hint of amused admiration in his blue glance.

"Still the same Perditta, I see," he commented dryly, "ever eager to have your own way — the only difference is that now you cajole, when a few years ago you would have fought."

"Jane gave Will into my care — "

"She asked you to care for both her children, which you have done."

"And grown fond of Will in the doing! Oh, Robert, let him stay here. He's an affectionate boy and I've won his love and trust. You must see that it would ruin the work of years if you took him away from the life he knows." I put a hand pleadingly on his arm. "Let me keep him," I begged.

The silence grew while he considered all the aspects of the case and I waited with bated breath for his decision. At last he covered my hand with his and turning to me, looked into my anxious face.

"I think Jane would have wished it," he said, smiling faintly as though at a painful memory, but the thought occurred to me that his smile held more of relief than sorrow and I found myself suddenly wondering how I could ever have thought I loved him.

Robert must have caught something of my thought, for he flushed slightly and looked away, his mouth suddenly tight.

"You may despise me, Perditta, but the knowledge of an idiot son is hard to bear. I could have put him away and refused to acknowledge him — at least I have not done that."

"No," I agreed, suddenly realizing how much it must have cost to mention Will to his coolly autocratic wife. "Leave him to me and start a new family. Hawks' Hill is in need of children's voices to bring it back to life."

Evidently he took my advice for having sent for his wife's children, he proceeded to do his best to fill his nursery. Lady Varley duly presented him with a new babe each year. Not all survived the dangerous months of infancy or escaped the plagues which visited us upon occasion but before long I could look upon his string of tall, thin faced children with envy. My fight for Will came to naught for very soon he was carried off by a cold which the other children withstood with ease.

The years passed on with very little to disturb the pleasant routine of our ordered life, but one day in the early summer about ten years after Jane's death a man rode through our gate and sitting his thin, knock-kneed old horse wearily, crossed his wrists on the pommel of his saddle and stared at the house.

I had been sitting in the window, to catch the light for my work, but now I put down my needle watching the shabby figure with puzzled curiosity. A black cloak, almost green with age and wear, covered his shoulders and what I could see of his breeches and doublet matched it in age and appearance. Long white hair hung to his shoulders, fluttering in the wind, topped by a limp steeple-crowned hat. But when he raised his head and I saw his face, tanned brown like a Moor, I started to my feet, catching my breath and pressing my hands against my heart that threatened to leap out of my bodice.

Scattering coloured silks and materials

heedlessly, I picked up my skirts and ran to the front door, dragging it open with fumbling hands, only to pause, irresolute, on the top step.

"Dudley?" I asked, unbelievingly. *Dudley?*

The man swung himself to the ground and sweeping the hat from his head, advanced towards me, his eyes on my face. For a moment we stared at each other.

"Perditta," he said, a wintry smile crossing his face and somewhat chilled by his manner I refrained from my first impulse to throw myself into his arms.

The tale he told was amazing; his ship, instead of sinking as we had supposed, had been driven before a storm far beyond Drake's fleet, until dismasted and uncontrollable she had been boarded by a Turkish galley and all her crew taken prisoner. Since then, until a few months ago, Dudley had worked as a slave, rowing the huge ship for his heathen masters and he showed us the manacle scars around his wrists. About his actual experiences he would say little, but I had only to look at him to see how the experience had changed him. When I had last seen him he had been a youth, saddened by his father's death but still eager for life and full of confidence and hope; now he appeared older than his years, quiet and introverted. His brown face, save when he spoke when some of the old vitality lighted it, was guarded and remote and his bony, tanned fingers toyed almost incessantly with the buttons on his doublet as though his hands were used to being occupied.

He seemed unmoved by Jane's death and I reflected that they had never been close and that it was thirteen years since he had seen his sister.

"Hawks' Hill went to her husband of course," said Conn. "I am not sure of the legal position . . ."

"No matter," Dudley said indifferently. "I have managed so long without possessions that I find they have little interest for me now."

I was to find how true his words were in the days that followed. A tailor came out from Alton, but Dudley showed no interest in his new clothes, standing impatiently while he was measured and asking for the plainest, darkest material. In his choice of bedchamber he was the same, refusing the best room, taking instead a long, low attic under the roof, bare of both furnishing and comfort.

"I have no need for luxury," he said, seeing my anxious face. "I have managed so long with bare boards, that I cannot sleep if I am too comfortable." He looked about the attic with low windows set under the eaves and touched the plain wooden table and chair. "I shall be content here, Perditta. Don't worry over me."

I frowned at the austere truckle bed, which was all he had allowed me to provide and twitched a corner of the coverlet into place.

"You've changed," I said, sighing.

"It's only to be expected," he agreed. "The years age us all. I'm a man now, not the youth you knew."

But over the next few weeks I was to learn that it was more than the lost years that had altered my cousin. His whole attitude seemed to have changed; if he had not still borne the likeness I remembered, I would have thought him a stranger. He shunned company, even Conn's and mine, keeping much to his room or spending many hours roaming the countryside, his solitary figure in his flapping black cloak reminding me of a crow as I watched him from the window.

"He's trouble, that one," observed Linnet, following my gaze.

"What do you mean?" I asked sharply, wondering if she had inherited her grandmother's powers.

"He'll cause trouble, that's all," she said. "I wish he'd go away."

Linnet had grown into a comely woman, something more than a servant and I allowed her many liberties but now I told her to remember of whom she spoke and quickly sent her about her duties. Despite my words I was inclined to agree with her, all the more so, perhaps, because I could not account for my unease.

Then came news which drove all else from my mind. A message arrived from Dame Allis to say that the Queen, who was making her annual progress, would stay overnight at Summer Ho and that the local gentle families were to be invited to meet her. My heart pounded at the news and I held out the letter to Conn, waiting for his reaction.

"So — you'll meet her at last," he said, quietly.

"I saw her when I was a child."

"This time you are a woman grown and able to use your judgement."

Even Dudley seemed interested in the Royal visitor and proclaimed himself willing to pay her homage. I was surprised by the gleam of excitement in his eyes — not having supposed him a loyalist — and said so.

His teeth showed in a brief smile. "My loyalty would astound you, cousin," he answered and my unease settled on my shoulders and slithered chill down my spine.

The next weeks were spent in an orgy of preparations. Dame Allis asking for many recipes from my mother's book and my advice upon other things, not that she needed or heeded it, she asked merely out of friendship and I was grateful for her thoughtfulness. I chose a satin gown of rust with a cream underskirt and slashings to the long puffed sleeves. For the first time I was to have a wired collar that rose like a fan behind my head and my stiff farthingale was a wider one than I had ever owned before, making movement difficult until I learned to take the tiny, stately steps that Lady Varley trod so daintily.

Dudley had been persuaded to wear a black velvet suit in place of the fustian he usually preferred but still I wished for some means of brightening his sombre appearance as I dressed in my finery. Taking out the Queen's pearls, my eyes fell upon a heavy silver collar, patterned with red enamel that had belonged to Jane and I knew that it was what I had been looking for. All the servants had been given a holiday to walk across the fields and see the royal visitor, so with a hasty explanation to Conn, I took it and quickly mounted the stairs to Dudley's room.

The stairs were steep and many, and before I reached the top I had to pause to regain my breath. As I did so an unexpected sound reached my ears. A soft murmuring chant came from the room above and at once I was back in my uncle's house all those years ago. For a second I listened while the hair rose on the back of my neck, then lifting my heavy skirts, I crept upwards.

The door was unlatched and I had only to push gently for it to open slightly affording me a view of the room beyond. Dudley knelt beside the table, his hands clasped and his eyes closed in fervent prayer. About his shoulders hung a satin stole and on the table stood various Catholic vessels, while before the silver cross and as though dedicated to it, lay a serviceable steel dagger, its polished blade gleaming blue against the white cloth that covered the improvised altar.

I must have made an involuntary movement, for my wide skirts caught the door sending it crashing against the wall. Instantly and with a litheness I had not suspected, Dudley was on his feet and had sprung towards me. His fingers closed over my arm and I was jerked into the room.

"You are a *priest!*" was all I could say and he nodded, impatient with my foolishness.

"I've an idea your husband suspects as much," he said, "but he was a sympathizer and helped us . . . perhaps he can be persuaded to do so again."

I stared at the dagger, a horrid suspicion forming in my brain and looked up to find that Dudley had read my thoughts.

"You are going to kill the Queen!" I gasped.

"My life shall be sacrificed for the one true religion," he said. "If I send that Protestant murderess to Hell, my death shall be remembered forevermore by the Catholic church and eternal masses said for my soul."

His eyes glittered fanatically and I stared at him, horror stricken. "You're mad," I cried.

"I was," he said simply, "after ten years on that damned galley I was mad and all the other slaves with me. Then, like angels from Heaven a Spanish galleon rescued us and I swore to give my life to the church in gratitude. It took me nearly three years to train and take my vows as a priest . . . and all those years I've longed for this day when I can avenge my father and rid the world of the Protestant she-devil."

"What an ambitious gentleman you are," remarked Conn, calmly pushing the door wide and stepping into the room.

For a moment the two men stared at each other, their hands not far from the swords they wore at their hips.

"Doubtless you heard what I was saying to my cousin," observed Dudley, his voice calm, but I could see the velvet of his doublet rose a little faster than was normal. "Are you with me?"

"To kill the Queen?" Conn slowly shook his head. "I never *was* with you . . . How do you think so many of your plans were known? I was Walsingham's man and supplied him with information — you could say that Mary Stuart's fall was due to me."

Dudley snarled in rage and took a quick step away from me. At once Conn was between us and as his arm swept me aside, I realized the reason behind his indiscretion.

"Go down stairs, Perditta," he said evenly. "I'll join you in a few minutes

— when this matter is settled." While I stood irresolute, he turned back to the other man. "With the reason behind your return made known, your plot must fail. Will you surrender yourself to me?"

For answer Dudley reached to his side and drew his sword, falling back on one foot and assuming a defensive position. As Conn's sword and dagger scraped free of their sheaths, both men had forgotten my presence and circled each other warily looking for an opening.

The steel clashed together, ringing loudly in the long room. Their blows lacked the finesse I had seen in practise fights, replaced by a grim determination that filled me with fear. I knew neither would give in. They would fight until one was dead. For a while it seemed Conn would win, he was taller and the better swordsman, but then I saw that Dudley was fighting with total disregard for himself, pushing his sparse body to unknown limits. Sweat had broken out on both men's faces and their breath rasped in their heaving chests. Suddenly I knew that Conn was done, I could see the effort it took him to lift his leaden arm as he blocked Dudley's frantic blows.

Retreating, I knocked against the table and suddenly remembered its burden. Snatching up the dagger I circled the fighting men seeking an opportunity, while they were so engrossed that neither was aware of my intention. Recalling the hard learned lessons of my youth, I aimed at the muscles of Dudley's sword arm, but as I struck, he turned and received the blow full in his left side.

Astonishment crossed his face, he hung poised for a moment and then slowly slid to the floor.

"Dear God, I've killed him!" I cried and would have gone down on my knees beside him, but Conn forestalled me, feeling in the black doublet for a heart beat.

"He's alive," he said briefly. "You must go to Summer Ho and make excuses for me, while I see him on his way."

For a moment I hesitated, but one look at Conn's grim expression told me that I had best obey him and heedless of my protests he bundled me out of the house and on to my horse.

All my life I had wanted to meet the Queen, but now that the wish was within my grasp I found that I was more concerned with other things. My daughters and I made our curtseys, but save for an impression of a magnificently gowned and jewelled woman with hooded eyes and a red wig, I have little recollection of the event, my mind being taken up with the happenings at Galliard's Hay.

Conn rode to meet us, joining us as the grey of evening began to take the colour from the countryside.

"Dudley was called away," he said as I raised my eyebrows in query and went on speaking loud enough for our companions to hear. "His mother sent for him and he left at once for France."

Behind me I heard Linnet sigh with open relief and looking round I saw the same emotion on many faces, which surprised me for I had not realized that my cousin had not been popular.

"Did he really go?" I asked when we were alone. "I — thought I had — "

Conn took me in a comforting embrace. "Think no more of him," he urged.

"Take my word that he will trouble you no more."

Later I realized that he had not answered my question and as the weeks and months passed I knew that for my own peace of mind I would never ask it again and all thoughts of Dudley were firmly locked away. Once I thought I saw his black cloaked figure in the trees beyond the garden and my heart thudded unpleasantly, but at my second glance the woods were empty and thankfully I knew I had been mistaken.

Imperceptibly Conn and I slid into middle age; our youth had gone without our realizing its passing. His shoulders were as straight, but my hair had lost its brightness, otherwise the years treated us kindly. The new century was born and then came two events that shook our peaceful existence.

Queen Elizabeth died and Robert Varley brought me her last gift, a miniature picture of herself, in a jewelled setting such as only Nicholas Hilliard could fashion, and on the piece of paper folded round it, in crabbed shaky writing were the words, 'to my dear daughter.'

"She meant Goddaughter, of course," I whispered.

"Of course," he agreed and said no more, then or ever.

And surprisingly, after sixteen fallow years I found myself pregnant again. The girls, who were already thinking of husbands themselves, were full of excitement at the prospect, while Conn was unashamedly delighted.

"A boy this time," he cried, catching me up in a bear hug and as quickly setting me down with exaggerated caution.

"A boy this time," I promised happily and put aside all thoughts of my age or the length of time since I had borne a child. Reaching up I stroked Conn's cheek, my heart in my eyes for him to see. "This time you shall have your son as proof of the love I bear you," I said softly and went into his arms as eagerly as a girl meeting her lover, knowing that whatever the future might hold, Conn and I had had the best of lives together.

Thanking the fate that had ordained that we meet, I sent up a silent prayer that Conn would be given the son he longed for to fill his declining years with all the hopes and ambitions of youth and for myself I asked that the babe should be cast in the image of his father that I might have another bold, black-haired man to love.

THE END

TO FIGHT THE WILD
Rod Ansell and Rachel Percy

Lost in uncharted Australian bush, Rod Ansell survived by hunting and trapping wild animals, improvising shelter and using all the bushman's skills he knew.

COROMANDEL
Pat Barr

India in the 1830s is a hot, uncomfortable place, where the East India Company still rules. Amelia and her new husband find themselves caught up in the animosities which seethe between the old order and the new.

THE SMALL PARTY
Lillian Beckwith

A frightening journey to safety begins for Ruth and her small party as their island is caught up in the dangers of armed insurrection.

NURSE ALICE IN LOVE
Theresa Charles

Accepting the post of nurse to little Fernie Sherrod, Alice Everton could not guess at the romance, suspense and danger which lay ahead at the Sherrod's isolated estate.

POIROT INVESTIGATES
Agatha Christie

Two things bind these eleven stories together — the brilliance and uncanny skill of the diminutive Belgian detective, and the stupidity of his Watson-like partner, Captain Hastings.

LET LOOSE THE TIGERS
Josephine Cox

Queenie promised to find the long-lost son of the frail, elderly murderess, Hannah Jason. But her enquiries threatened to unlock the cage where crucial secrets had long been held captive.

TIGER TIGER
Frank Ryan

A young man involved in drugs is found murdered. This is the first event which will draw Detective Inspector Sandy Woodings into a whirlpool of murder and deceit.

CAROLINE MINUSCULE
Andrew Taylor

Caroline Minuscule, a medieval script, is the first clue to the whereabouts of a cache of diamonds. The search becomes a deadly kind of fairy story in which several murders have an other-worldly quality.

LONG CHAIN OF DEATH
Sarah Wolf

During the Second World War four American teenagers from the same town join the Army together. Forty-two years later, the son of one of the soldiers realises that someone is systematically wiping out the families of the four men.

THE LISTERDALE MYSTERY
Agatha Christie

Twelve short stories ranging from the light-hearted to the macabre, diverse mysteries ingeniously and plausibly contrived and convincingly unravelled.

TO BE LOVED
Lynne Collins

Andrew married the woman he had always loved despite the knowledge that Sarah married him for reasons of her own. So much heartache could have been avoided if only he had known how vital it was to be loved.

ACCUSED NURSE
Jane Converse

Paula found herself accused of a crime which could cost her her job, her nurse's reputation, and even the man she loved, unless the truth came to light.

THE PLEASURES OF AGE
Robert Morley

The author, British stage and screen star, now eighty, is enjoying the pleasures of age. He has drawn on his experiences to write this witty, entertaining and informative book.

THE VINEGAR SEED
Maureen Peters

The first book in a trilogy which follows the exploits of two sisters who leave Ireland in 1861 to seek their fortune in England.

A VERY PAROCHIAL MURDER
John Wainwright

A mugging in the genteel seaside town turned to murder when the victim died. Then the body of a young tearaway is washed ashore and Detective Inspector Lyle is determined that a second killing will not go unpunished.

DEATH ON A HOT SUMMER NIGHT
Anne Infante

Micky Douglas is either accident-prone or someone is trying to kill him. He finds himself caught in a desperate race to save his ex-wife and others from a ruthless gang.

HOLD DOWN A SHADOW
Geoffrey Jenkins

Maluti Rider, with the help of four of the world's most wanted men, is determined to destroy the Katse Dam and release a killer flood.

THAT NICE MISS SMITH
Nigel Morland

A reconstruction and reassessment of the trial in 1857 of Madeleine Smith, who was acquitted by a verdict of Not Proven of poisoning her lover, Emile L'Angelier.

SEASONS OF MY LIFE
Hannah Hauxwell
and Barry Cockcroft

The story of Hannah Hauxwell's struggle to survive on a desolate farm in the Yorkshire Dales with little money, no electricity and no running water.

TAKING OVER
Shirley Lowe and Angela Ince

A witty insight into what happens when women take over in the boardroom and their husbands take over chores, children and chickenpox.

AFTER MIDNIGHT STORIES,
The Fourth Book Of

A collection of sixteen of the best of today's ghost stories, all different in style and approach but all combining to give the reader that special midnight shiver.

DEATH TRAIN
Robert Byrne

The tale of a freight train out of control and leaking a paralytic nerve gas that turns America's West into a scene of chemical catastrophe in which whole towns are rendered helpless.

THE ADVENTURE OF THE CHRISTMAS PUDDING
Agatha Christie

In the introduction to this short story collection the author wrote "This book of Christmas fare may be described as 'The Chef's Selection'. I am the Chef!"

RETURN TO BALANDRA
Grace Driver

Returning to her Caribbean island home, Suzanne looks forward to being with her parents again, but most of all she longs to see Wim van Branden, a coffee planter she has known all her life.

SKINWALKERS
Tony Hillerman

The peace of the land between the sacred mountains is shattered by three murders. Is a 'skinwalker', one who has rejected the harmony of the Navajo way, the murderer?

A PARTICULAR PLACE
Mary Hocking

How is Michael Hoath, newly arrived vicar of St. Hilary's, to meet the demands of his flock and his strained marriage? Further complications follow when he falls hopelessly in love with a married parishioner.

A MATTER OF MISCHIEF
Evelyn Hood

A saga of the weaving folk in 18th century Scotland. Physician Gavin Knox was desperately seeking a cure for the pox that ravaged the slums of Glasgow and Paisley, but his adored wife, Margaret, stood in the way.

DEAD SPIT
Janet Edmonds

Government vet Linus Rintoul attempts to solve a mystery which plunges him into the esoteric world of pedigree dogs, murder and terrorism, and Crufts Dog Show proves to be far more exciting than he had bargained for . . .

A BARROW IN THE BROADWAY
Pamela Evans

Adopted by the Gordillo family, Rosie Goodson watched their business grow from a street barrow to a chain of supermarkets. But passion, bitterness and her unhappy marriage aliented her from them.

THE GOLD AND THE DROSS
Eleanor Farnes

Lorna found it hard to make ends meet for herself and her mother and then by chance she met two men — one a famous author and one a rich banker. But could she really expect to be happy with either man?

THE SONG OF THE PINES
Christina Green

Taken to a Greek island as substitute for David Nicholas's secretary, Annie quickly falls prey to the island's charms and to the charms of both Marcus, the Greek, and David himself.

GOODBYE DOCTOR GARLAND
Marjorie Harte

The story of a woman doctor who gave too much to her profession and almost lost her personal happiness.

DIGBY
Pamela Hill

Welcomed at courts throughout Europe, Kenelm Digby was the particular favourite of the Queen of France, who wanted him to be her lover, but the beautiful Venetia was the mainspring of his life.

PREJUDICED WITNESS
Dilys Gater

Fleur Rowley finds when she leaves London for her 'author's retreat' in the wilds of North Wales that she is drawn, in spite of herself, into an old tragedy.

GENTLE TYRANT
Lucy Gillen

Working as Ross McAdam's secretary, Laura couldn't imagine why his bitchy ex-wife should see her as a rival.

DEAR CAPRICE
Juliet Gray

Clifford Fortune married Caprice but his brother, Luke, knew the marriage was a mistake. He could allow himself to love Caprice blindly but that would be betraying his own brother.

IN PALE BATTALIONS
Robert Goddard

Leonora Galloway has waited all her life to learn the truth about her father, slain on the Somme before she was born, the truth about the death of her mother and the mystery of 'an unsolved wartime murder.

A DREAM FOR TOMORROW
Grace Goodwin

In her new position as resident nurse at Coombe Magna, Karen Stevens has to bear the emnity of the beautiful Lisa, secretary to the doctor-on-call.

AFTER EMMA
Sheila Hocken

Following the author's previous auto-biographies — EMMA & I, and EMMA & Co., she relates more of the hilarious (and sometimes despairing) antics of her guide dogs.

LEAVE IT TO THE HANGMAN
Bill Knox

Dope, dynamite, guns, currency — whatever it was John Kilburn and his son Pat had known how to get it in or out of England, if the price was right. But their luck changed when one of them killed a cop.

A VIOLENT END
Emma Page

To Chief Inspector Kelsey there was no shortage of suspects when Karen Boland was murdered, and that was before he discovered that she stood to inherit substantially at twenty-one.

SILENCE IN HANOVER CLOSE
Anne Perry

In 1884 Robert York is found brutally murdered at his home in Hanover Close. When, three years later, Inspector Pitt is asked to investigate, the murder remains unsolved.

A RARE BENEDICTINE
Ellis Peters

Three vintage tales of medieval intrigue and treachery featuring the author's monastic sleuth Brother Cadfael.

POIROT'S EARLY CASES
Agatha Christie

In this collection of eighteen stories, Hercule Poirot begins his celebrated career in crime.

THE SILVER LINK
— THE SILKEN LIE
Lynn Granger

Elspeth is determined to preserve her Scottish heritage and the Elliot name, but running Everanlea, a large hill farm, presents problems.